QUAKE

PATRICK CARMAN

QUAKE

SCHOLASTIC INC.

ISBN 978-1-338-03834-7

12 11 10 9 8 7 6 5 4 3 2 1   16 17 18 19 20 21

Printed in the U.S.A.   40

First Scholastic printing, March 2016

Typography by Joel Tippie

For Katherine
Mover of Mountains

Contents

I used to draw things and make little notes but I don't do that anymore. I'm too tired. I've let so many details slip away these past months because living is a lot of work or because I grew out of writing things down or I just got lazy. I woke up one day and realized I wasn't writing things down anymore. I guess it happens.

I used to ask my mom what she remembered about being my age, and the answers were all broad strokes of runny paint. I got nothing out of those conversations. I'm worried I'll forget everything that's happened to me, too. I'll get old and looking back I'll find shades of color that run into each other, no sharp lines of detail.

I'm lying next to my one and only, my Dylan. He's asleep and the soft light of my Tablet is setting the cool sheets aglow. I'm writing down the crisp lines of how I arrived here, nothing more.

For a while I lived in the shadow of the Western State. If for some unforeseen reason the States disappear, they are not hard to describe. They are utopias, or so I'm told. In my part of the world there are two: the Western State and the Eastern State. They grow larger every day, eating whatever space lies in front of them. They spread like an oil slick, hundreds of millions of people living inside. They are not inherently evil, I don't think. But once entered, they are a thing I could never turn back from. I see the States in a very specific way: my time before going inside, and my time after. I have a strong feeling that if I ever do go inside I will change into something I don't want to be. My resolve will crumble. My distinctiveness will fade into the many. I fear this outcome.

Outside the States is an empty, abandoned space. I think only 1 percent of humanity lives out here with me, something like that. It can feel lonely outside, forgotten.

Hotspur Chance, Wade Quinn, Clara Quinn: these are my enemies. These three are responsible for the death of my parents and my best friend. They also killed Dylan's mother. They seek to destroy us, too. They fuel the fight inside me.

There are only four second pulses in the world. The first pulse gives them the ability to move almost *anything with the power of the mind, including themselves. The second pulse deflects all things. These four people are close to indestructible, but not quite. Each one has a weakness, a Kryptonite.*

I am one of these four; Dylan is another. Wade and Clara Quinn are the other two. We are at war with one another.

My only weakness is titanium. If someone made a titanium bullet and shot me in the head with it, I'd be in real trouble. Any other bullet would bounce off my second pulse like a Ping-Pong ball. Dylan's weakness is concrete and stone. The Quinns, being twins, have the same weakness: living stuff either in the ground or freshly pulled and still alive, like trees and weeds and roots. I think really fresh dirt might not agree with them, either, but that hasn't been proven. I once tangled Clara and Wade Quinn inside a web of ivy and watched them struggle. That was a good day.

There are single pulses, too. Single pulses can move things with their mind, but they can't deflect something coming at them, like a car or the pavement. I was a single pulse once. Looking back now I realize what a dangerous time that was. I would use my mind to make myself fly, never thinking about how easily I could crash. It's no small miracle I lived long enough to discover my second pulse.

Hotspur Chance is a single pulse. This makes him vulnerable, which is why they hide him. He's the smartest man on earth, the designer of the States, and also ruthless. I can't decide if I hate him or not. I think I do. He has a singular vision about life on this planet, and he'll do anything to see it through. I can appreciate that kind of resolve. The problem is that the people I love stand between him and this vision of his. Okay, yeah, I hate Hotspur Chance. He didn't kill my best friend; that was Clara Quinn. He didn't kill my parents; that was Wade Quinn. But he brought these two monsters into the world and let them do whatever it took to free him from a prison inside the Western State. He's the head of the beast, the brains, the heartless center.

Hotspur also created the Intels. There are even fewer of them left in the world. I think Clara and Hawk are the only ones. It's a very good thing Hawk is on our side, because Intels are nearly as smart as Hotspur. They are brilliant thinkers with photographic memories. They learn new skills much faster than I do. They analyze, calculate, and hold information like supercomputers. Hawk has created a lot of high-tech gadgetry for us, like the sound ring. I have one. So do Dylan, Hawk, and Clooger. If I press the lobe on my ear and speak, they all hear me in their heads no matter where they are. If I don't press, they don't hear. Elegant and useful. We drive around in a modified Hummer that floats a few inches off the ground like a hovercraft. So yeah, Hawk makes really cool stuff. We'd all be dead without him.

We made a serious run at killing the Quinns and we came close, but in the end we became misunderstood fugitives. The Quinns freed Hotspur and hid him away somewhere. Dylan's mom, our leader, was killed.

Clooger, our single-pulse leader, has a plan to hide us away, too. He's old military, strong as a horse, and overprotective. I'm going along with his plan to run away and heal up for now, but no one—not Clooger or Dylan or Hawk—is going to stop me from what I have to do.

My fight will never be over until the Quinns and Hotspur Chance are gone for good.

Now I'm going to tuck inside the arms of the one person I trust completely and fall asleep. When I wake up the rest of my life will unfold and I probably won't write any of it down. At least I got this far.

Chapter 1

Flight

Hawk's breath fogged the glass of his Tablet as dawn broke on the world outside. He turned to Clooger, whose wide nose had turned a pale shade of pink in the chill of morning, and said a single word.

"Incoming."

Clooger's black eyebrow went up and he dug a finger into his ear. The up and down of the mountain drive had left him feeling as if he was underwater.

"Here or there?" Clooger asked.

"There. And stay on your side of the rig. Whatever you're finding on that ill-fated ear expedition is probably nuclear."

Clooger pulled his finger out and examined it. "Better make contact."

"You sure?" Hawk asked. "With this much activity so close, who knows? We might blow their cover."

Clooger leaned his huge shoulder closer to Hawk and looked at the Tablet.

"Cover's already blown. Call 'em."

Hawk nodded. At fifteen he was scrawny for his age, but next to Clooger's colossal frame, he looked like a four-year-old.

"Dylan? Faith? Can you hear me?"

Hawk's small voice traveled into the sound ring as he searched for Dylan and Faith. He pressed hard on the lobe of his ear and wondered if the communication system he'd invented had been damaged.

"They're coming for you, Dylan. Tell me you're hearing this. Get out of the house. Get out now."

Still no answer.

"Why didn't you see this sooner?" Clooger asked. He was tougher on Hawk than anyone, but he loved the kid like his own son.

Hawk glanced at Clooger as if he was crazy.

"We both woke up thirty seconds ago. How much faster were you thinking?" asked Hawk.

"You should have an alarm on that Tablet for situations like this."

"At least Wade and Clara aren't out there." Hawk

scanned his Tablet again. "I don't see them anywhere."

Clooger was starting to worry, flexing his muscles nervously as he gripped the steering wheel. He blamed himself for their falling asleep, but they'd been up for thirty-six hours in a row. It wasn't as if they could stay awake forever. "We should have slept in shifts instead of simultaneously passing out from exhaustion. I should have known better."

"They've got maybe three minutes, Cloog," Hawk said. His fingers danced across the screen of the Tablet he held in his hand. "I don't know how this group found the safe house, but they did."

"At least the town is zeroed," Clooger said, stepping lightly on the accelerator. The HumGee hovered a few inches off the deserted mountain road, turning back and forth between fir trees. "How many?"

"A full unit of Western State military army." Hawk paused and looked at Clooger. He was glad to have the big guy at his side. "Air and ground. They've surrounded the house."

Clooger sniffed the air like a wolf and stared intently out the window. He pressed the sound ring embedded in his ear and yelled.

"Dylan, if you can hear me, move! Now!"

Hawk tweaked out in his seat at the booming sound of Clooger's voice and banged his head on the ceiling of the HumGee. His Tablet went airborne and hit the dashboard, instantly shrinking to its handheld size as it tumbled to the floor.

"Think you could warn me when you're planning on going nuclear?"

But that was Clooger—a bull in a china shop—and he was never going to change.

"What is it?" Dylan asked. He was finally awake, rubbing the sleep out of his eyes in a room filled with darkness and narrow slits of light.

Faith rolled over and looked at Dylan. She felt her side, hoping she'd find it healed from Gretchen's titanium dart, a dart that had nearly ended her life a day earlier.

"It's too late," Hawk pressed in. "They've surrounded the house. And I mean *really* surrounded it."

"Could they hide?" Clooger asked. He didn't press his sound ring, so only Hawk could hear him ask the question.

"Not a chance. Those troops have heat-seeking tech. Unless Dylan and Faith can seriously play dead, they'll have to make a run for it."

"If you guys get caught now it'll be a disaster," Clooger said, pressing his sound ring. He veered the HumGee back onto the road and gunned it. "Head into Oregon. I'll relay more instructions once you figure out how to evade everything the Western State can throw at you. Whatever you do, don't get caught."

"Faith, how are you feeling?" Hawk asked, pressing into the sound ring. He used his Tablet to set the auto-pilot on the HumGee and nodded for Clooger to let the steering wheel go.

"Ready to roll," Faith said. She was standing next to the bed in a T-shirt and underwear, nothing else. When she lifted her shirt along the side of her body, Dylan saw in the faint light that the wound had healed into a jagged scar.

"Nice birthmark," Dylan said as he pulled a shirt over his head and stepped off onto the floor on her side. He pulled her in close and edged back toward the bed.

Faith pressed her sound ring and pushed Dylan away with a smirk. "This is escape time, not make-out time," she whispered.

"I'm good as new, plus one badass scar," Faith said. "And my abs on that side feel like I just did a thousand sit-ups. I can roll."

"Excellent," Hawk said. "I had a feeling your body would regenerate very quickly. Glad I was right about that."

Faith pulled on her pants and a second, long-sleeve shirt. She picked her Tablet up off the nightstand, sliding it into the back pocket of her jeans.

"Figure out how to get away from the army outside

and back into hiding," Clooger said. "We'll guide you from here."

"Okay, first things to know," Hawk said, scanning his Tablet for data. "You've got two dozen armed flyers with jet packs surrounding the house. They'll be able to keep up, and they may know you can't be stopped with bullets or bombs. It's hard to say *how* much they know. Overhead you've got a half-dozen hovercraft. Those are fast and very nimble in the air. And they have space for a lot of weaponry."

"Like nets," Clooger reminded Dylan and Faith. "If they know about your powers, they'll know they need to trap you in order to stop you. Remember that."

"Okay, we got it," Dylan said. He looked at Faith, pulled her close again, kissed her.

"You sure about this?" Faith asked.

"Does it matter?"

Dylan kissed her, longer this time. When Faith pulled away and saw the longing in Dylan's eyes, she thought of how much she wanted to stay in the safe house, just the two of them. But she knew their escape from reality was over. They both did.

"No, it doesn't matter if you're sure, not really."

"Then let's get this party started."

Before either of them could pull the curtains, the glass in the window exploded inward and a can of tear gas hit the floor, flooding the room with eye-stinging smoke. They both heard the sound of the front door downstairs being forced open with a ramrod as armed men entered and began shouting instructions.

"My system doesn't much like this tear gas. You?" Faith asked.

"Can't say that I love it," Dylan agreed. They weren't sure whether their second pulses would protect them from poisonous gas; they'd never dealt with it before. No sense taking chances. Dylan went first, then Faith, flying out the window and up into the sky. They stopped and hung in the air over the house long enough to see the trouble they were up against. Men wearing sleek jet packs were already taking off, heading toward them, and firing a barrage of bullets.

"Pretty cool tech," Dylan said, surveying the armed forces. "I'd love to get my hands on one of those jet packs and take it apart piece by piece. Imagine what Hawk could cook up with the parts?"

"Too bad they don't have any interest in capturing us. These guys are aiming to kill," Faith said, trying to keep Dylan from geeking out, as he sometimes did at the most inappropriate times. Faith had long understood that things like jet packs and flying saucers set off even the least nerdy guys she'd ever met. Ogling this kind of modern technology was in their DNA. She glanced skyward as she and Dylan flew toward the Oregon border, bullets pinging harmlessly off their second-pulse shields. Overhead she saw the circle of hovercrafts, each of them thirty feet in diameter. They looked like oversized bumper boats, round and flat with one pilot sitting in the center.

"Let's see if we can outrun them," Dylan said. "That would be the easiest way out. And I'm curious what kind of speed these things can do."

Faith nodded and they went into high gear, arching up toward the cloud line. But the bullets and rocket grenades kept coming and the men in jet suits stayed tight on their heels. The hovercraft were even faster, encircling them from every side, firing at will.

"Open space isn't working!" Faith said. "Try close to the ground?"

Dylan nodded and they dove toward an abandoned street with houses on both sides.

Several hundred miles away, Clooger and Hawk were keeping track of the action as they drove.

"Spread out, you two," Clooger said, pressing his sound ring. He was leaning toward Hawk, watching heat signatures on the Tablet as the autopilot swerved them back and forth down a dusty road. "Make them choose who to follow!"

The HumGee went fast into a turn and pitched sharply to the right, throwing Hawk into the door. Clooger's weight followed, smashing Hawk as if they

QUAKE ◀ ◀ ◀

were on a shoulder-crushing fair ride.

"Buckle up, big guy! You're killing me here."

"Don't be such a wimp."

"I'm not a wimp. You're huge, bro!"

While Hawk and Clooger waited for the next hairpin turn, Faith picked up an abandoned car with her mind and threw it over her head. The men in jet packs swerved admirably, but when they looked back, Faith had picked up ten more cars. She turned on the troops and they all stopped in midair, watching.

"Stop following me," she said. Faith had a way of saying things like this that could turn the most hardened army veteran toward home. But these guys were either stupid or crazy or both. The troops all moved forward slightly, firing off a whole new round of bullets and blasters.

"Don't say I didn't warn you, because I did. I warned you."

Faith moved the cars into a long horizontal line in front of her and then pushed them forward one at a time like pendants stuck together on a chain. By the time they started reaching their intended target, the cars were traveling at a hundred-plus miles an hour, spreading out and clobbering everything in their path. The troops bounced like bowling pins, spinning wildly out of control as the jet packs malfunctioned and pushed

15 ◀ ◀ ◀

them all over the sky. The cars continued their journey, slamming into houses and streets on the ground as the flying Western State troops tried to right themselves in midair.

Dylan was a quarter mile to Faith's left, dealing with the hovercrafts, all of which had decided to follow him.

"Clooger was right on the money—these things have net bombs," Dylan said, dodging hard to one side as a bowling ball–sized projectile headed his way. When it was within twenty feet of where Dylan had been stationed, it burst open like a shotgun shell full of lead pellets, splaying out a wide net with golf ball–sized weights around its perimeter. A long wire connected the net to the hovercraft, and when the net missed its target, it curled back into a ball and returned to where it had come.

"We need cooler weapons," Dylan said, pressing his sound ring so Hawk could hear. "You gotta see this, Hawk."

"You do realize it's killing me not seeing this stuff up close?" Hawk said as he turned toward Clooger. He pressed his sound ring. "Grab whatever you can!"

Dylan nodded to himself, but he knew it would be a fool's errand trying to separate a Western State flyer from his equipment. He looked down and uprooted an entire house with his mind, raising it into the air from below as dirt and debris crashed to the ground. All six hovercrafts fired net bombs, surrounding Dylan as they exploded in a circle around him. Dylan shot into the air, raising the house as he went. The nets were beyond sticky, covered in something that adhered to whatever they touched. Dylan heard the pilots screaming, *"Release! Release!"* But they weren't fast enough. Dylan pushed the house back toward the ground, pulling the hovercrafts down with it. By the time the lines were all cut, it was too late and all six pilots had to abandon ship, taking to their emergency parachutes and brandishing sidearms.

"Let's make a run for it," Faith said. "Stay low to the ground, out of sight."

The jet-pack troopers were barely getting their bearings again, and the hovercraft pilots were totally out of the fight. Only two troopers followed Faith and Dylan into the trees.

"A couple of stragglers and we should be clear." Faith pressed into her sound ring. She looked at Dylan, saw what he was considering. "Don't even think about it. You are not going back there for a hovercraft or a jet pack. Let it go."

"Sorry, Hawk." Dylan smiled. "I'd have done it for you, but Faith is a little more rational than me."

Dylan moved in close, wrapping an arm around Faith's waist. They kissed and Faith felt Dylan smiling. She loved it when this happened. To touch his lips to hers when he was this happy, to *feel* his happiness and know it was because of how much he loved her—it was everything, all she needed, all she wanted.

"Man, it would have been fun parting out one of those jet packs," Hawk said, his voice all excited and bummed out at the same time.

"It was a search mission," Clooger said. "Now that they've found you they'll send more. You need to move fast and find some cover."

"Head for the Columbia Gorge," Hawk pressed into the sound ring. "A million acres of trees along there. They'll never be able to track you."

"Still two on your tail, but they're falling back," Clooger added.

The HumGee turned suddenly to the left, barely missing a cliff wall as it continued down a winding forest-service road somewhere on the border of Oregon and Idaho. Hawk lowered his shoulder and used the gravity of the turn to slam Clooger as hard as he could, but his shoulder missed and Hawk face-planted into a wall of Cloog.

"I almost feel sorry for you. *Almost*," Clooger said, laughing softly as Hawk felt around his head for missing parts.

"I think you broke my face."

Clooger glanced at Hawk and gave him a playful shove.

"All in a day's work for a military man, right, kid?"

Hawk went right back to his Tablet, all business. "Let's get these two out of harm's way before another State armada shows up. It's all clear for the moment."

But Hawk was about to find out how wrong he was.

Faith and Dylan were far from in the clear.

Chapter 2

Gun Smoke

Both parties settled into their respective journeys for the next twenty minutes, covering a lot of ground fast. Faith and Dylan were especially quick, finding themselves flying low over the dense forest near the Columbia Gorge in no time.

"So you're really not going to tell us where we're going?" Dylan asked, pressing his sound ring.

Clooger had been asked where the new hideout was more times than he could count. Everyone wanted to know. But it was secret in part for a very personal reason, and he didn't want to take any chances until he absolutely had to.

"You're heading in the right direction."

That was all Clooger would say as they kept on, deeper into the green and blue of the Northwest.

Faith kept glancing back, wondering if the two jet-packed stragglers were still behind them, but she hadn't seen anyone chasing for a while.

"Hawk, any reading on the two that were following us?" Faith pressed in.

Hawk had been keeping an eye on the whole region for any signs of movement, but the task was complicated. He could easily track Faith and Dylan because they were locked into a sketchy GPS system he'd created. Spotting a large movement of troops or something big like a jetliner—those were things he could do. But small enemy objects, not that much bigger than a large bird? Almost impossible. The fact that the HumGee was at top speed, whirling through the empty world at over a hundred miles an hour, didn't help matters.

"I can only get a lock on you and Dylan within a few-mile radius," Hawk said. "If I could latch onto the State grid it would help, but that's risky. They might detect a signal coming in. I'm catching the network where I can, looping through old Wi-Fi zones. It's a mess out here."

As they broke through the trees and Dylan saw the wide expanse of the Columbia River, he decided it was time to let loose a little. They were free of the Western State, the Quinns, the weight of responsibility that had gotten so heavy. It might all return without warning, and Dylan wanted to remember this moment.

He turned out of the forested hills and over an abandoned road that wound along the edge of the broad river. Faith followed close behind, tailing Dylan's every move. When they reached the water it was unusually calm, like a sheet of reflective glass. Dylan flew low, a foot off the surface, bending the face of the river into a soft ripple.

"It's beautiful," Faith said from behind him. "There's a heaviness, like it's a thousand feet deep."

The Columbia was so wide and slow moving that on a rare, windless day it could look as if it weren't moving at all. Dylan put a hand down and touched the cool water. It sprayed Faith head-on before she could move out of the way.

"Oops," Dylan said, but he knew what he was doing. "I thought you were faster than that."

Faith wiped the liquid out of her eyes and, with a determined look, blasted past Dylan and returned the favor. Dylan did a somersault over Faith's head and cannon-balled hard, soaking Faith all over again. He surfaced like a dolphin, made some weird porpoise noises, and dove back in.

Faith laughed and circled the water, waiting for Dylan to return, but he stayed under.

"Come on, Merman. Get what's coming to you."

Faith flew quickly back and forth, then rose higher

into the air for a better look. Her field of vision widened to include a dam several miles off to her right and the looming presence of Mount Hood to her left. She glanced back over the road and into the forest, and that was when Faith saw something moving on the tree line: two people, gliding effortlessly along the tops of the cedars.

"Dylan," Faith said, moving closer to the water once more. She pressed her sound ring. "Dylan! Get up here. We have company."

Dylan erupted out of the river, not like a dolphin this time. Like a killer whale, straight up and full of purpose. He came alongside Faith and ran his hands through soaked hair.

Hawk pressed his sound ring and spoke. "Wait, something's not right. These two aren't presenting like they've got jet packs. The heat signatures are all wrong."

"But they're wearing Western State military uniforms," Dylan said, wiping the water from his face and eyes. Even with the distance between them there was no mistaking the white shirts, the red pants.

"It's them," Faith said. She knew it before anyone else did. She just *knew*. "It's Wade and Clara. They've found us."

"Hawk? You agree?" Dylan asked. He wasn't ready to believe the Quinns had somehow tracked them down.

"It's possible they're tapped into the Western State

security protocols. If they're monitoring intel, they'd know about the raid at the safe house."

"Or maybe they were there all along," Faith said, inching toward the tree line. Her eyes narrowed and her look went ice-cold. A lock of blond hair tumbled in front of her eyes and she pushed it back.

"Take it easy, Faith," Dylan said. He knew that look, had seen it a hundred times before. "This is not the time for all-out war with the Quinns. We need to regroup, heal up. We need to run."

Faith retied her hair in a ponytail with a rubber band she'd found at the safe house and looked at Dylan. "There's never a good time to run."

"Follow the river until you reach the dam," Clooger yelled into his sound ring. "There's a lot of debris along the way: boulders and abandoned cars along the road. You can use those to keep them back. Stay on the water; it's the safest place right now. At least if you crash you'll hit the river."

"Is it just me, or did he forget about drowning?" Faith asked as she watched Dylan arch his back, stretching his chest and arm muscles.

"Captain of the swim team in middle school. I can hold my breath for like ten minutes."

They both knew Dylan hadn't even *gone* to middle school. He'd been too busy preparing for situations exactly like this one his entire life.

"Don't underestimate these two," Faith said. "They're State Games athletes, remember?"

Dylan could see what Faith was thinking as he came closer, water dripping down his neck and arms. He moved closer still, within a few inches of her face, and saw the old rage in her eyes.

"Let's at least keep some distance between us," Dylan said. "Come on. You're not ready to rock and roll just yet."

"You underestimate me," Faith said, still staring off toward the line of trees at the oncoming threat. Wade and Clara Quinn seemed to understand they'd been seen. The two of them were now moving fast toward Dylan and Faith.

"Rage is like rocket fuel, Dylan. Those two subhumans flying toward us? They killed my parents. They killed your mom. They would have taken out a million people in the Western State. They're not just criminals, Dylan. They're mass murderers. They're a plague."

Dylan took her by the shoulders. Another thirty seconds and the Quinns would be on them. Then it would be all-out war.

"We're going to get this done, Faith. I promise. No one is more focused on that than I am. But this isn't the time, and they're not the target."

"They *are* the target. They always have been."

"But they're not the *primary* target," Dylan said,

taking her hand and pulling her in the direction of the distant dam. "Hotspur Chance. He's the one who has to go. If we don't get rid of him he'll spawn more Wades and Claras. We have to cut the head off this thing, and we can't do that if one of us doesn't live through a war with Wade and Quinn out here in the open. It's going to take both of us, Faith. You know that. And you know this is too risky."

"Why aren't you guys moving?" Hawk asked, pressing into the sound ring.

Clooger was less patient. "MOVE!"

Clooger's authoritative voice had the effect of snapping Faith out of her dark thoughts and she began to follow Dylan's lead. Within a few seconds they were traveling at over a hundred miles an hour over the smooth surface of the river.

The Quinns had already gotten close enough to start some trouble. A line of graffiti-riddled freight cars lay on their sides in a ravine on the far side of the river. They rose into the air like a clanging necklace of pendants attached on a chain.

"Always with the trains, these two," Faith said.

"Be ready to do some dodging," Dylan said as he and Faith both picked up every abandoned car they saw and hurled them in the direction of the Quinns. There was metal flying everywhere. Cars, vans, and semitrucks flew over the water, forcing the Quinns to dodge and spin. It slowed them down, but Dylan and Faith were also thrown up and down and back and forth as the train cars swirled in the shape of a twister.

"That is the nastiest shit storm I have *ever* seen," Faith yelled over the sound of metal crashing into metal. The Quinns were aiming the twister of train cars back and forth, forcing Dylan and Faith to move out of its way and pushing them toward the Quinns.

"Let's get on the other side of this thing," Dylan said. "See if we can outrun them!"

Even Faith was starting to see that a full-scale battle out in the open was going to be hard to win against these two foes. She turned back and watched as Wade Quinn didn't bother moving out of the way of a Greyhound bus flying right at him. Instead he took it head-on, punching through the middle and leaving a four-foot hole from roof to carriage. The bus crashed into the water, rolled over a few times on the surface, and sank into the river. The look on Wade's face was a hybrid dance of power and pleasure. Faith felt sure he lived for this kind of thing, the hunting down and killing of his enemies.

"See the downed power lines running off the dam?" Hawk asked into the sound ring. "Those might prove useful."

As they approached the wide expanse of the dam, Faith saw what Hawk was talking about: cables as long as a football field slithered back and forth on the surface of the water, black and lithe and empty of life.

"They attach to generators along the wall of the dam, distributing electricity when the turbines run," Hawk continued. "This power source hasn't been operational for a long time, but see if you can open the turbine gates with your mind. If you can, water will begin flowing through and that should send an electric current through the cables."

"And that would send a million volts of electricity into the water," Clooger said into his sound ring.

"Why the hell would we want to do that?" Dylan asked. He looked at Faith, wondering if she thought the idea was as crazy as he did.

"Because *they* won't know the water is juiced," Faith said. "But we will. We just need to make sure we're either far enough downstream or out of the water in time."

Dylan nodded and smiled. "You distract them, I'll see if I can fire these things up."

"Be careful, Dylan," Faith said as she started toward the train-car twister charging angrily in her direction. "Remember, concrete is not your friend."

"Watch out for titanium darts," Dylan yelled back. "I can handle myself."

Faith's one and only weakness was titanium. Any titanium weapon could get through her defenses—a dart, an arrow, a titanium-covered bullet; it was her

Achilles' heel. Rock and stone were Dylan's, and for the Quinns it was earth and living things. It didn't matter how many cars or buses Faith Daniels threw at Clara and Wade Quinn. The only thing it would do was slow them down. None of that kind of weaponry could harm them. She'd have a better chance of injuring them with a dozen roses.

When Faith and Dylan split up, Wade pushed the train-car twister directly toward Dylan and the dam. Clara went straight for Faith and abandoned all other effort. Faith pulled away from the water and toward the line of trees, where she could put Clara at risk of coming into contact with a living thing from the earth. Trees were Faith's friends when Clara was after her. As she approached the tree line she heard a distinct sound—a gunshot—and looking back saw that Clara Quinn had pulled out a handheld weapon.

She's got a gun, Faith thought. *And if she's smart she's got titanium bullets.*

There was no doubt about Clara's intelligence. She was an Intel just like Hawk, smarter than Faith and Dylan put together. Faith increased her speed and passed the first of many tall fir trees, dodging back and forth. She heard a series of shots fired and felt a bullet barely miss its target as it traveled past her ear. Faith took an extremely hard right before Clara entered the forest, turning back in the direction of the river, and came in behind Clara. She pushed herself to top speed, slamming into Clara's back as she was starting to turn. The gun fired off three more rounds, sending titanium bullets pinging off of tree trunks.

Faith held Clara's arms at her side. She'd never been this close with a person who had caused her so much pain. It wasn't what Faith thought it would be. She could smell a light, flowery perfume on Clara's skin. She could imagine Clara's striking eyes, her nose flaring with anger. It was harder to hurt someone when you were holding on to her, feeling her skin against your own.

Faith aimed for the side of the biggest tree she could find and tried not to think of what she was about to do. When Clara's face and body hit the side of the tree, it was as if she was crashing into pavement. The impact took Faith's breath away but she held on, sliding Clara up the side of the trunk, shearing off tree limbs as Clara's face did the work of a bark remover in a lumberyard. Faith held on to Clara's close-cropped blond hair, pushing her face harder into the tree as they traveled upward.

"Drop the gun!" Faith said, because that was the real objective here: get the weapon out of Clara's hand.

Clara screamed as the tree burned her face, the bark scraping off skin like sandpaper. Clara reeled around on Faith, slapping her across the face with the gun. The gun slipped free and tumbled end over end through the trees, landing in thick underbrush.

Faith saw that she'd marred Clara's perfect face—the whole left side was covered in deep gashes, blood pouring out. Her stomach lurched—*Did I really do this to another human being?*—but she pushed on, holding Clara against the tree and sliding her upward along the trunk, tearing long, whiplike scratches into her back. Faith could feel herself beginning to lose her resolve. It didn't matter how much pain Clara had caused her. She watched Clara breathe deeply, saw her tongue lash at the blood on her face, and wasn't sure she could keep going.

"Faith! Where are you?"

It was Hawk in the sound ring, and he sounded alarmed.

"If you can hear me, get to Dylan. Get to Dylan now!"

Faith and Clara stared at each other, inches apart, neither of them precisely sure of what would come next.

"If you're not going to finish what you started, you better run," Clara said, boring down on Faith with her sharp eyes. "Because I am one angry bitch right now."

"I will never run from you," Faith said. She pushed Clara harder against the tree and held her weakened adversary still.

"Faith! If you're there, get to the dam," Clooger

yelled into the sound ring. "Now!"

Clara laughed through her nose smugly, but it lasted only a second before she started taunting Faith again. "You're going to pay for messing up my perfect face. It's going to cost you. Hope it was worth the thrill."

Faith gave Clara one last shove, pushing her to the side this time, sending her careening through the trees deeper into forest.

She pressed her sound ring.

"I'm coming, Dylan."

Faith saw the gun on the forest floor and picked it up with her mind. It landed heavy in the palm of her hand. When she cleared the forest and saw the dam, she understood immediately why Dylan was in trouble. He'd opened the turbines and water was churning through in frothy white tubes. The power lines were sparking and dancing on the water's surface like huge electrified snakes, but that wasn't the really dangerous thing. Dylan was standing on the top of the dam and the train-car twister was headed right for him. Wade was pushing it forward and down, spinning it faster, and it was going to crash right on top of Dylan before Faith could get there.

"Faith, we need to seriously run," Dylan said into the sound ring. "I'm going to have to dive into the water on the other side of the dam. It's the only place he won't be able to see me. Take to the sky! We'll find each other."

But Faith had no intention of leaving Dylan's side, and besides, she could feel Clara's presence behind her. Clara was on the chase, bleeding and angry.

The twister of train cars hit the dam like a twisting metal bomb, blowing a giant hole into a wall of concrete that had stood for a century. The dam burst as freight cars flew in every direction. Chunks of concrete and rebar filled the path of water pouring down the river, and somewhere in all that metal and stone, Dylan was trying to swim away unseen.

Faith pulled a truck-sized boulder from the bottom of the river and launched it at Wade, slamming him in the back and sending him spinning wildly through the air. When he recovered and saw that Faith was trapped between himself and Clara, he smiled that terrible smile of his.

I'm in control now, the smile said. *There are no rocks big enough to stop me.*

Faith knew instinctively when she had met her match. Dylan was right. Now she really did have to get out of there if she could.

If she tried to fly away, they would eventually catch her or she'd end up in the middle of a battalion of Western State troops out searching for her. There was only one way out, one hope now that she was alone between two of the most dangerous people in the world.

She dove, hard and fast, into the Columbia River.

Untold megawattage coursing through the river stunned her senses. Her second pulse protected her from harm, but it still felt like diving into a pool of broken glass, cutting every square inch of her skin. She opened her eyes and saw the waves of blue electricity pulsing down her sides as the force of the current pulled her forward toward the broken dam. This was water and debris that had been held in place for decades, unmoved. But it was moving now. *Everything* was moving.

Sunken cars, trees, boulders, slabs of concrete, bathtubs, sheets of metal—anything and everything that had ever been dumped into this slow-moving stretch of water was now tumbling toward the gaping hole of a dam that was no longer holding back the water.

Faith felt the stinging-jellyfish sensation of electricity covering her skin as she came up for air and saw how close she was to the dam. Something slammed into her from behind and she went under, rolling uncontrolled with the flow of a river gone mad.

When she cleared the dam itself, the electric current began to weaken. Each time she bobbed up for more air she glanced quickly overhead. She could see Wade and Clara against the blue sky behind her, searching the surface for signs of life.

She took another breath, dove under, and let the water carry her away.

Chapter 3

Poison Flowers

Faith awoke to the sound of a scream. At first she thought the voice was inside of a dream she was having, but when her eyes were open and the sound persisted, she sat up, throwing the covers from her bed with the power of her mind. She focused on a baseball bat she kept next to the door and it came to her, landing with a sharp sound in the palms of her hands.

Her next thought was of the sound ring.

It must be coming from inside the ring. Someone is in trouble.

She'd gotten so used to hearing familiar voices in her head that it was sometimes hard to distinguish them from her own thoughts.

She pressed her earlobe, and that was when she felt a sharp pain and remembered Hawk had removed it. He'd used a scary-looking pair of needle-nosed pliers that looked as if they were designed to reach inside someone's head and pull out all sorts of stuff that should be left alone. Hawk had removed the sound rings from everyone's ears.

"Repairs and upgrades," he'd said.

Faith hadn't bothered to ask what the upgrades might be as blood ran down the side of her neck and she punched him in the chest. Hawk was never very forthcoming about how much things were going to hurt, and removing the sound ring had *really* stung. Faith didn't even want to think about what putting an upgraded version back into her head was going to feel like. That was the thing about a second pulse: she had to let her guard down in order to allow something like the sound ring inside. And when she did that, she felt pain just like everyone else.

The scream kept on, accompanied by the sound of an ax hitting a door over and over again. Faith shook her head awake as she walked down a cedar-walled hallway and arrived at a door three down from her own. By then she was aware of what the sound was. She'd heard it many times before.

"Trying to catch a few z's," she said, tapping the bat

on the door several times. "Can you guys keep it down in there?"

All sound ended behind the door. There was some shuffling of feet, some giggling, and then the whispery voice of a girl.

"How come she goes to sleep so early?"

Faith turned the handle on the door with her mind and pushed it open with the bat. Dylan was sitting on the lone couch as if he'd been waiting for her to show up. Hawk sat on the floor of the small room, and there was a young girl of thirteen next to him. She had a round face and long, dark hair. Faith had quickly come to see the girl for the enigma she was: at once bored and full of mischief. One minute she was talkative, the next aloof. And she was especially nervous around boys at or near her own age. Hawk and Dylan were something altogether new, dangerous, exciting. Her name was Jade, which matched the color of her eyes.

"*Again?*" Faith asked. "How many times have you watched this movie?"

"A dozen," Hawk said. "No, eleven. Eleven times. Twelve if you count this time. So 11.735 times, give or take."

Faith rolled her eyes and mumbled, "Too much information."

She flopped down on the battered cloth couch next

to Dylan and put her head on his shoulder.

"Have you fixed anything else yet? Scary movies scare me."

"It's more than a scary movie. *The Shining* is a masterpiece," Dylan said in a sleepy, half-zoned-out voice. "This Stanley Kubrick guy was off-the-charts intelligent. If I didn't know better, I'd say he was an Intel. This movie is layered."

"*So* layered," Hawk added. "It's a mind-blower."

"Deeeeeeeep," Jade said, holding back a laugh with her delicate hand.

"I'd definitely say some minds are blown in here," added Faith. She averted her eyes from the screen, pulling closer to Dylan and smelling the woodsy pine of the flannel shirt he was wearing.

"Did you roll around in the forest today? You smell awesome," she said.

Jade took notice of the interaction and leaned approximately one centimeter in Hawk's direction, sniffing the air.

Dylan held his sleeve to his nose and breathed in deep. "It does smell awesome. This *place* is awesome. Let's never leave."

"The shirt smelled like that when you found it in the cedar chest?" Faith asked.

"Yeah," Dylan admitted.

She put a hand on his chest and kissed him on the

QUAKE ◄ ◄ ◄

neck, furrowing in like a cat on a cold night.

Dylan loved old movies and he wished more of them worked. "These VHS tapes are falling apart. Options are limited until Hawk figures out a restoration process for the classics. The tapes are basically disintegrating."

"Yup, total annihilation," Hawk said. "It was bad mass storage to begin with."

Faith picked her head up off Dylan's shoulder and stared at him zombielike.

"I know what to get you for your birthday," she said. "Old scary movies. You can watch, I'll snuggle. Win-win."

Faith found *The Shining*—what little of it she had watched—highly disturbing. The story was about a writer who goes insane and tries to murder his family. And the setting?

Jade crinkled her nose. "How can you not love *The Shining*? It was filmed here."

"That makes it double scary for a romantic-comedy girl like me."

It was true. *The Shining* had been filmed in the very location where Faith Daniels was hiding out with the tattered remains of a resistance: Timberline Lodge, up a long, abandoned road on Mount Hood. Faith and Dylan had tumbled three miles down the Columbia River before escaping unseen into the woods. Dylan had been hit by chunks of concrete blown free from the dam as

39 ◄ ◄ ◄

he tried to swim away, but he'd survived. They'd stayed to the woods after that, guided up the mountain by Clooger and Hawk, and here they were.

They'd been holed up in the lodge for over a week while the adults plotted and planned. The stakes were higher than they'd ever been now that Hotspur Chance was free, and it made Faith feel that they shouldn't be hiding out, that they should be *doing* something. But then she'd smell Dylan's shirt and think about the night at the safe house and wonder: *Could we just stay here, like forever, and never go back into the fray?*

The lodge was high enough up that she could see the very top of the mountain. It was a breathtaking peak half blanketed in snow, beautiful and wild, covered in jagged rocks and steep angles. She could stare at the peak for long moments, thinking of nothing at all, losing herself in its grandeur.

Timberline Lodge had been a ski resort before the States wiped everything out. The isolation of the place only made the movie they were watching more macabre. No one had been near the lodge in decades; at least that's what people in the States assumed. But Clooger's brother Carl and his daughter, Jade, had been living there for years. They never used Tablets, never went near the Western State. Carl lived off whatever the mountain gave him, hunting and gathering, and he liked it that way. They were an exceptionally rare breed, these two:

off the grid, totally undetected, unknown to the States by any assigned Tablet or known address. They were ghostlike apparitions outside the never-ending crawl of the State system.

"Who knew being a fugitive could be so relaxing?" Dylan said, smiling as he ran his fingers through Faith's long hair and signaled Hawk to restart the VCR.

"It can get a little boring," Faith added.

"It's a fine line, boredom and relaxation," Hawk said. "Depends on your DNA, your personality. Me, I'm never bored. I'm always thinking."

"Me neither," Jade agreed.

Faith noticed Hawk's eyes light up and was reminded once more that she was no longer Hawk's crush. He had finally moved on.

"Without our Tablets there aren't a lot of choices," Hawk reminded Faith, tapping the remote control as the VCR whirled back to life.

The screaming started up again.

"She really has a set of pipes," Faith said. "I bet they can hear her screaming in the Western State."

The crazy writer's wife in the movie was holding a butcher knife, which was only fair since the writer was holding an ax. She was also 100 percent unhinged.

Dylan put his warm hand over Faith's ear as she thought about all the shows she wanted to watch but couldn't. New shows and games were accessible only through their Tablets, but streaming content on Tablets sent a signal. Even with Hawk's knack for hacking into the code in order to keep them hidden, they were among the most wanted people in the world. They had to stay off the grid unless it was absolutely necessary for some vital piece of information, like coordinates or maps or intel. Movies and TV shows didn't qualify as risk-worthy, so whatever VHS tapes still worked were all they had to choose from.

The entire usable collection was made up of *Star Wars*, a murky-looking *Titanic*, the second half of *Ferris Bueller's Day Off*, *The Breakfast Club*, *Sixteen Candles* (recently added to the dead pile), and *The Shining*.

The Shining had cult status among the group.

"You just have to lean into it," Hawk said. He'd become weirdly obsessed with *The Shining*. "Like Dylan said, Stanley Kubrick was probably a pre-Intel or whatever. He was something else."

"Like Hotspur Chance?" Faith asked, perking up a little. Hotspur was their mortal enemy, and as far as they knew, he was plotting to destroy the States and usher in some kind of new world order. Intel had been hard to come by in the intervening days, which was driving Faith crazy.

The screen on the old TV was filled with Jack Nicholson's maniacally grinning face as he peered through a door. Faith had seen only snippets of the movie, because they were always stopping it to debate the meaning of things like the twins, the colors, the numbers, the hand-holding, and the endless loop the boy rode on his Big Wheel.

"Doesn't this movie bother you?" Faith asked Jade. Faith had been playing big sister since they'd arrived, a decision that sometimes worked and other times didn't. Jade was unpredictable, so when she turned those stunning green eyes toward the couch, Faith wasn't sure what to expect.

"They're almost to the hedge maze," Jade said. "Scariest part."

Jade got up off the floor and sat next to Faith. That left Hawk alone on the throw rug with the remote. He eyed the couch, calculating whether he could fit in the space that remained.

"Don't even try it," Dylan said. "This sucker is maxed out."

Hawk went back to watching the movie and Faith pulled Jade in close.

"I've seen it like a hundred times," Jade whispered over the screams, leaning harder into Faith. "But it always scares me just the same."

Faith couldn't help but think about how this innocent girl had never been off the mountain and had no idea how scary life could really get.

"Stop it there," Dylan said.

Hawk fumbled with the controller and had to rewind a little bit. He was nervous around Jade. The scene had shifted to a snowy night outside and a little boy was hiding behind a snowplow.

"It's the dead of winter," Dylan said, "but you can't see his breath. Do you think that's on purpose or a mistake?"

"I think I'm going back to bed," Faith said.

She kissed Dylan and wandered out of the room with her baseball bat, wondering how it was that she could be so tuned out to something everyone else seemed so tuned into. *It's them, right?* she kept telling herself. *Or possibly it's me.* Either way, she couldn't watch parts of that movie without imagining a nightmare in the making.

The lodge was an abandoned outpost, full of old snowboards, guest rooms, and long hallways. Almost all the rooms were empty, but it didn't make the lodge feel haunted or lonely. Faith liked it up here, away from the world and all its problems. She liked to think she preferred the thrill of being in the fight, but Faith was starting to feel something new on top of this mountain: she had found a place she could imagine calling home.

She walked down the long hallway lined with old pictures of people skiing. The images looked as if they were from a million years ago, everyone laughing and posing in their powder pants and goofy goggles. She wondered if such emotions existed inside the States, because carefree was the last thing Faith could imagine ever feeling again. Too much had happened. Too many people had been taken from her. Her world had moved irreversibly beyond lighthearted. She could never get that back, not that she could recall ever feeling that way to begin with.

Faith heard a sound behind her, a faint creak on floorboards marred with age-old ski-boot scratches. She turned, instinctively wielding the bat.

"I've seen that movie more than twelve times."

It was Jade, whose forehead didn't even reach Faith's shoulders. Jade tiptoed a few steps closer, rubbing her hands together nervously.

Faith played along. "How many times have you seen it?"

Jade shrugged. "I've been up here my whole life with no Tablet and eight movies on those old tapes. How many times do you think I've seen it?"

"Too many?"

Jade shrugged and looked at the floor again, a habit that made her appear younger than she was, a vestige of childhood she didn't know how to throw off. "Hawk likes it."

Faith smiled and moved a step closer. "And you like Hawk?"

Jade laughed nervously, quietly. She glanced back

toward the door to the TV room as if her biggest secret had just been revealed and someone might hear. She turned back to Faith with a knowing look and shrugged once more.

Faith lifted her shoulders, too, raising an eyebrow.

"Your secret's safe with me," Faith said, although she knew it was obvious to everyone that Jade and Hawk were circling each other.

"Can you tell me something about him? Something that might, you know, help me?"

Faith knew that Jade was desperate for help navigating her first crush. And so, while she knew it would hurt, Faith let her memory drift back to the Dr. Seuss book she had torn to shreds, and further still to Liz and Hawk on a night alone in a hidden library full of books. The memories bloomed inside her like poison flowers, fast and all-consuming, drawing her down into darkness. Faith pushed the memories down, deeper than they were before, and told herself not to go searching for them ever again.

"There are a lot of old books here, the kind that are printed," Faith said. "Give him one of those, and make it one that will tell him something about you."

"But that's so boring," Jade said. "He's been out there doing all this amazing stuff. He's seen *everything*. Why would he want some old book from a place the world has forgotten about?"

It was a hard thing to explain and Faith was desperate to move her mind away from where this conversation had taken her. "Trust me on this one. Hawk has a thing for real books. You'll thank me later . . ."

Jade eyed Faith suspiciously and began backpedaling as the sound of *The Shining* poured out into the hallway. A moment later she was gone and Faith continued alone, trying not to think about the things she'd dredged up, things that scared her a lot more than a movie about a madman loose in a ski lodge.

Faith turned a corner and walked right into the barrel chest of a giant moving quickly down the hall. She jumped back and swung the bat, but Clooger was fast. He caught the end in his hand.

"You need to mellow out," Clooger said. "Look first, *then* swing."

"Sorry, I—"

"Don't worry about it. I'm glad you're awake," Clooger said. "Get Hawk and Dylan and meet me at the fire."

Clooger let go of the bat and started to leave.

"What is it? What's going on?" Faith asked.

She didn't think Clooger was going to answer as he ran his hand over the growing stubble on his head, but then he did.

"It's time to finish what we started."

Chapter 4

Prisoner One

In the largest room of the lodge a gathering of leather couches encircled a raging fire where six people sat together. This was all that remained of a frayed resistance in a world on the brink of catastrophe.

Faith scanned the faces and landed on Clooger's brother. She wondered how much Carl knew, how committed he was, what his role would be. Dylan and Hawk and Clooger had proven themselves, but Carl was a wild card with a child, and Faith thought being a parent might complicate things. Would he grab Jade and run the second that trouble showed up? As for Jade, she was naïve and caught in the snare of first love. The biggest risk she represented was distracting Hawk at a time when they needed him most.

There was something else unusual about Carl: he made Clooger look like an out-of-shape middle-aged couch potato. They stood facing each other from opposite sides of the small gathering. Both had the same frame to work with, but what was built on those bones was astonishingly different. Clooger was huge and strong as an ox, but he was soft around the edges. If Carl weren't standing beside him, it would be easy to say Clooger was the biggest, strongest person Faith had ever seen. But Carl *was* standing next to Clooger as the fire crackled behind them in the dim light, and that made all the difference.

Carl's neck was as wide as his oversized head, a head that was covered in long waves of raven-black hair. His back and chest were broad and solid like a refrigerator, but it was his bare arms that demanded attention. If biceps were guns, these things were rocket launchers: bigger around than most people's thighs and endlessly ripped with muscle.

Carl lifted weights relentlessly in the lodge gymnasium and read old gun magazines as if they were the Holy Bible. He was armed to the teeth with weaponry— Lugers and knives holstered in six different places up and down his body armor. There was a rumor going around that he had a stash of munitions fit for an army, but Faith had seen only what Carl wore around the lodge all day and night.

"Okay, listen up, everyone," Clooger began. He had abandoned his beloved trench coat in favor of a blue and gray flannel shirt and jeans, but he still had the sawed-off shotgun strapped to his left leg.

"We've finally gotten some serious intel from one of the sleeper cells in the Western State. Hawk, maps."

"Roger that."

Clooger's military background had rubbed off on Hawk, and they sometimes spoke in what Dylan and Faith called "command and answer."

"What sleeper cells?" Dylan asked. "I thought we were it, the whole resistance."

Clooger looked at his brother, nodded once, and Carl spoke.

"It appears Meredith had a small group on the inside—how high up we don't know. Hell, we don't even know who they are or if the intel is accurate. But it's something, a thread."

"It's accurate," Clooger said.

Carl looked at his brother, flexed his guns. "Says you."

The two of them were friendly rivals, Carl younger by a couple of years. There was no way Cloog was backing down. A staring contest ensued until Jade intervened.

"Mellow out, you two. We're on the same side, remember?"

Clooger got right up in Carl's grill.

"I'll mellow out if he does," Clooger said.

Faith knew it was all about the facts with Clooger, so she zeroed in on what they knew. "How about you tell us what you heard and how the information got here. We can all decide if the intel is solid or not."

Both men seemed to view this as a practical way to save face. They both faked a punch at each other and neither flinched. Clooger faced the group.

"A contact sequence for this outpost was established twelve years ago when Carl and Jade moved up here. The lodge was a last resort, a final out if we had no place else to go. I thought only Meredith and I knew the sequence, but she must have told at least one other person."

"She was always like that," Dylan said, a slight edge to his voice. "The center of a wheel, connected to spokes that didn't know anything about one another. I have to hand it to her; she knew how to keep secrets better than all of us put together."

Carl picked up the thread.

"When we established this station we went all retro, totally untraceable. We're talking FM radio wired up to an ultra-high-frequency carrier wave. The only way to even get on that wave is to have the right equipment.

We're talking massively specific, ancient technology."

"So you're saying it works like radio used to work, but it's on a frequency almost no one knows about?" Hawk asked.

"Bingo," Carl said, pointing his massively muscle-bound arm at Hawk. Faith was starting to get that Carl was an off-the-grid geek-junkie extraordinaire. If it was hacked or stolen, do-it-yourself or cobbled together from random parts, or shot with your own gun and cooked over a fire on wood from a tree you cut down, or, better yet, blew out of the ground with a homemade explosive, Carl loved it.

"I built only three systems," Carl went on. "Mine, Cloog's, Meredith's. So how is there a sleeper cell out there contacting us with intel?"

Faith jumped in before another argument could break out between the two biggest guys in the room.

"Okay, so someone else knows how to get on the frequency and has the right equipment to do it," Faith said. She looked at Clooger. "How's that possible? And either way, what are the odds this communication system has fallen into the wrong hands?"

She and everyone else watched as Hawk projected a three-dimensional holographic map of the United States into the air in the middle of the room.

"The signal was sent from inside the Western State, that much we know," Clooger said. "Millions of people have gone in over the past decade, and plenty of them were drifters before that. The comm unit is small, easy to conceal."

"So you're saying Meredith gave hers to someone?" asked Hawk.

Clooger nodded. "And that someone is finally using it."

Clooger took two steps toward the fireplace and picked up an oblong device. It looked like something out of a 1950s science-fiction movie: clear Plexiglas encasing a row of diodes and bulbs and wires all soldered to a motherboard. The entire thing was half the size of a brick.

"The Plexiglas is solar powered; it absorbs heat and converts it into electricity."

"That's a Hotspur Chance invention," Dylan said. "Kind of cool we get to use it against him now."

"Okay, so maybe the entire thing isn't old-school, but the stuff inside is," Carl said sheepishly.

"If a signal comes in, it gets recorded to a micro drive and the red light goes on. That way you don't have to monitor it twenty-four/seven. You just watch for the light."

A thumbnail-sized red light inside the device was throbbing on and off like a tiny beating heart.

"Eleven years," Carl said. "Eleven years and not a single red-light day. Now it's lighting up like a Christmas tree, two alerts in as many weeks. First you guys, and now this. It makes me nervous."

"This sleeper cell had one purpose, I'm sure of it," Clooger went on. "To feed us intel from inside the States. The message we got verifies that. If they were trying to pinpoint our location they would have asked for it, but they specifically told us not to respond. They don't know where we are and they're not going to know."

"So Meredith set up a sleeper cell inside the Western State and didn't tell anyone else about it," Faith said.

"They aren't sleeping anymore," Clooger said. "They're awake."

Clooger set his pocket-sized Tablet on top of the Plexiglas and tapped out a few commands. The room filled with the sound of a female voice.

"Prisoner One has escaped from maximum-security Western State detention zone. Message relay ordered. M4-ZTom unlock code 45.5.122.67. Do not respond to this feed. Terminating."

Silence fell on the room as the flames cast moving shadows across the walls and ceiling.

"Prisoner One," Hawk said. "Hotspur Chance, most wanted man."

"It's not a very clear message," Jade added.

"Is it all you have?" Faith asked Clooger. "It sounded as if we were supposed to unlock something else. Or maybe it's not even for us."

Clooger sighed. "It's something. It's a start."

"It might be a lot more than that."

Everyone pivoted in the direction of Hawk's voice.

"Let me see that thing," Hawk said, pointing to the device Clooger held in his hand. Clooger kept his Tablet and handed over the strange, clear block. Hawk peered inside, rotating the Plexiglas housing, until he found what he was looking for.

"Carl, can you open this up or is it vacuum sealed?"

"Depends," Carl answered. He pulled a large, hammer-like tool from his belt. "Are you going to want to use it again?"

Hawk took an even closer look at the device and saw that there was no way around breaking the outer shell. The items inside—the diodes and wires and bulbs— were all soldered directly into the bottom section of the casing. The only way in was to break it open.

"We have two, right?" Faith asked. She was worried about cutting off communication with everything and everyone. At least with one of these, she felt a small connection to the world outside the mountain. Carl nodded—*Yes, there's one other.*

"Hawk, what are you not telling us?" Dylan asked.

Hawk photographed the underside of the Plexiglas box with his Tablet, then set the box down and stretched his Tablet large. He enlarged and sharpened the photo, then held it out so everyone could see it, pointing to a rectangle. On the device itself, this rectangle was about as big as a baby tooth, but his Tablet had taken a high-definition picture and now it was blown up to fill the screen.

"This is the micro flash drive the voice message was recorded on," Hawk said. He leaned forward and a mop of brown hair covered half his face like a curtain. "I've read about these old Tom drives. These little guys could hold a terabyte of data. They were a revolution in their time."

"Is this what I think it is?" Faith asked.

"An M4-ZTom," Hawk said. "And if we can access it directly, then I'm guessing the passcode we were just given will unlock something hidden there."

"Hawk, I love that computerlike brain of yours," Dylan said. "You're a genius!"

Faith looked Dylan up and down, head to toe, and marveled at how this boy could carry the weight of the world and still take the time to compliment every-one around him. His dark hair was getting longer and he was letting his stubble grow out. He still wore the T-shirts and the jeans and the skater shoes, even in the mountains, but he was looking more like a grown man every day. He flashed a sideways smile at her and it felt as if they were one person, not two.

Hawk turned his attention to Jade and smiled as if

to say, *Not a big deal, I do this sort of thing all the time.* Jade smiled back at him, her gem-green eyes glancing back and forth between the floor and Hawk's face, but she kept her cool. It was hard not to be impressed with Hawk when he pulled off technological miracles.

Carl took the device back from Hawk and set it on the floor.

"You sure about this?" he asked no one in particular. Hearing no objections, he removed a foot-long buck knife from a leather sheath at his hip. He placed the tip on the Plexiglas box and hit the butt of the knife once with the hammer. The glass shattered with a sharp popping sound and Hawk leaned down with a pair of tweezers from a tech kit he kept in his cargo shorts.

"Nice shot, Carl," Jade marveled. "Not too hard, not too soft. You hit it just right."

"Nerds really do inherit the earth," Dylan whispered to Faith, putting a hand on her knee as they waited nervously.

"We got the best one," Faith added, loud enough for Hawk to hear her and see him crack a smile as he lifted the tiny object out of the mess Carl had made.

"Give me a minute here," Hawk said, holding the small M4-ZTom flash drive between the tongs. "I'll run it through my Tablet using a digital signal."

Everyone watched anxiously as Hawk took forever

figuring out how to connect old technology to new technology.

"We have to connect through a wireless signal developed after the chip was made—not easy," Hawk continued. "It's like driving a train on a freeway: a path that doesn't match the mode of transportation."

"This is what it will be like when the aliens invade," Faith joked. "They'll find our Tablets and break them apart after we've gone the way of the dinosaurs."

Jade leaned in closer to Hawk and he quietly told her everything he was doing. Dylan moved his broad shoulder close to Faith and the skin on their arms touched. He was seeing the same thing Faith was, two kids falling fast for each other. Faith smiled in a way that said, *That is adorable and dorky and perfect.*

"Got it!" Hawk finally said. "Someone read me that code again."

A terrible silence settled over the room as they realized no one had written the code down and the device had been broken into and taken apart.

Hawk shook his head. "I give you guys one simple job. Just one."

"No, wait, I got it!" Jade said. "45.5.7.122. I think."

"Are you sure?" Faith asked. "I thought there were more numbers than that."

Jade hated that she might be wrong about the code,

but she had to admit she wasn't 100 percent sure.

"It's okay, I think I can play it back," Hawk said. He took a deep breath and exhaled. "It'll just take me a minute. I hope."

With Hawk, a deep breath followed by the words "It'll just take me a minute" could mean four seconds or four hours. It was impossible to know which, and Clooger groaned. Luckily for everyone's sanity, this turned out to be a reasonably simple coding issue for an Intel like Hawk, and it was solved quickly.

"Chalk one up for the good guys," Carl said. "This kid is good."

The room filled with the sound of the message for a second time. There was more static in the transmission this time as it made its way across the divide of many years and several iterations of technology.

"Prisoner One has escaped from maximum-security Western State detention zone. Message relay ordered. M4-ZTom unlock code 45.5.122.67. Do not respond to this feed. Terminating."

"You were really close, Jade," Hawk said. "Only one number off. You've got an excellent memory. Definitely better than Clooger's."

Jade beamed with pride, brushing her dark hair back with a delicate hand as Hawk entered the full code into the drive—45.5.122.67.

There was a pause and a series of static waves that made everyone's heart sink, and then a voice almost all of them had heard before materialized in the room: Meredith, Dylan's mom and the former leader of the rebellion, was back from the grave.

> *If you're receiving this message, then I am dead.*
>
> *I'll give you a minute to let that sink in.*

There was a lengthy pause in the transmission and Faith remembered what a straight shooter Meredith had always been. She was the most matter-of-fact person Faith had ever met.

Faith looked at Dylan and found that he was staring at his shoes. She put her hand on his as Meredith's voice returned.

> *Hawk, I'm going to assume it was you who unlocked this message, which means you also know how to pause what I'm saying. I can still give orders, and I'm ordering you to pause this message until everyone who is still alive from the following list is present: Dylan, Faith, Clooger, Hawk, Carl, and Jade. You should all hear this information at the same time. That was what I intended.*

Hawk tapped his Tablet screen and the recording stopped. He looked up at all the stunned-into-silence faces in the room as if the decision to continue was not his own.

"All present and accounted for," Clooger replied with a distant kind of weariness in his voice. "Let it play."

"Sorry. I was just making sure we're good to go on this. Also double-checking I can stop it if I need to," Hawk said. He glanced around awkwardly. "I can stop it."

Hawk half smiled and tapped the screen again. When he did so, Jade leaned in closer to listen, their knees touching.

> *For the purposes of this transmission I will address everyone I named even if some of them are already dead.*
>
> *Carl, if you haven't told them about the sleeper already, tell them now.*
>
> *This would be the part where Hawk hits pause.*

Hawk pointed to the screen and let Jade tap the pause button and the two of them leaned even closer to each other. Faith couldn't help thinking how remarkable it was that love could blossom in the most difficult of times. It was, she thought then, the most powerful thing on earth.

"What's she talking about?" Clooger asked his brother. Clooger hated the idea of being on the outside of any information that involved the team.

Carl had been standing, but now he sat on the stone edge of the fireplace. The fire had softened to embers, but there was still an orange glow around Carl's enormous head and shoulders as he spoke.

"You remember Liz's boyfriend, Noah?"

Faith's head shot up. "Of course I remember Noah. He's all she talked about. What about him?"

It was hard for Faith to think about anything having to do with Liz, her first and only best friend. Any mention of Liz led right to the hammer crashing into her head and the rage and sadness boiled over. Faith gripped Dylan's hand tighter as she was reminded of what Clara Quinn had done.

"There's more to Noah than you all knew," Carl continued. "He's on our side, always has been, but it started with his parents. Noah's dad is deep Intel, as Meredith would say. He's got no pulse, so he can't protect himself. His only job is to be in there, digging up information and waiting in case one of us ends up inside the Western State. It's something he's good at. Think of him as an undercover information specialist. It's not likely very many people know about Meredith's death or would even know what her significance was if they did know. But Noah's dad can find his way inside

State-run information systems. He fed intel to Meredith all the time, whatever he could get to. Obviously she told him to send this message if he ever found out she was dead."

Carl did some counting in his head. "I guess it took Neal Gordon—that's Noah's dad's name—twelve days, give or take, to find out what you already knew. Meredith didn't live past the siege that let Hotspur Chance out of prison."

"How do you know all this?" Clooger asked, genuinely crushed by the idea that Carl would know more than he did.

"Like I said, Meredith spread things around, shared what she wanted with who she wanted. And she expected us to keep our secrets well. I'm sure you know plenty of stuff I don't have a clue about. Balances out."

"What if she knew something we didn't?" Jade asked.

Dylan was reminded once more of his mother's incredible capacity for secrecy. "Jade, I can promise you, Meredith knew *a lot* of things we don't know. That's the way she was, cagey. Even with us. Even with me, and I'm her son. Whatever message she's got for us, it's probably not information we already know, and it won't be good news."

"Never is," Faith agreed. "Maybe that's why she chose not to tell us everything."

Faith could feel the weight in the room getting heavier, the energy turning downbeat. "Let's listen to the recording, see what we've got. It might be nothing more than a sad good-bye. But if it is something more, we need to know about it."

"I wish Neal Gordon would have contacted us faster," Clooger said. "Hotspur Chance has had twelve days to get organized. That's time I'd like to have back."

Carl sighed heavily. "The war will still be here no matter how many days pass, brother. It always is."

"This is different," Clooger corrected, his gaze settling heavily on his brother. "You know it's different."

Faith let that sink in for a few seconds and realized it was true. She locked eyes with Dylan and felt his resolve to finish what they'd started. More than ever, she knew they would have to face whatever was coming together. She couldn't do it alone and neither could he. "Let's listen to what she has to say already," Jade pressed. "I've never even met Meredith and now I'm as curious as you guys are."

Clooger looked at Carl in a knowing sort of way, as if they both had to agree to this before they'd give the okay. Faith got the feeling that they were nervous about what might be said, which made her wonder if these two had secrets of their own they weren't telling.

"Let 'er rip," Carl said, nodding to Hawk. "And let the chips fall where they may."

Jade reached over and brushed her finger across the Tablet, and Meredith's voice returned.

> *I'm terrible at good-byes, especially recorded ones, but I have to say them.*
>
> *Good-bye, Dylan. I loved you; you made me proud. More than anyone else, you made me believe the world was worth saving.*
>
> *Good-bye, Clooger, my comfort and my shield. In a broken world, you gave me the strength to go on. Sorry if I'm revealing this secret unexpectedly, but this is my only chance and I'm taking it.*

Faith looked up at Clooger and saw that he was staring at Jade with a worried expression on his face. A second later she knew why.

> *Jade, I am your mother. I'm sure Clooger has been too nervous to tell you yet, and given his proclivity to finding himself in very dangerous situations, he might never have told you. Clooger is your father, young lady. If you didn't know that already, my apologies.*
>
> *Remember these things as you go through life:*
> *We loved you enough to get you out of harm's way before it was too late. You should be thankful for that. War is no place for a baby.*

*You have a half brother, Dylan, who is
probably also listening to this message. He was
five when you were born and we whisked you
away before he could see you. Dylan will keep you
safe, because he's a man now and a very good one.
Him you can trust.*

*Be good to Carl. He deserves it. No man ever
sacrificed so much for one child.*

*Secrets and lies are part of every life. While
I don't advise lying, sometimes it is necessary to
protect an innocent person.*

*If we'd kept you close by you'd almost certainly
be dead already. Be thankful that's not true.*

I thought of you. Always.

Hawk, pause. Let's take a break.

Hawk touched the screen and stopped the recording, stealing glances at everyone in the room but Jade.
"Okay, so that was awkward," he said.

"Sorry," Carl and Clooger said at once, having the
same thought at the same time.

Jade's expression softened. She didn't speak, but
Carl and Clooger could see by the way she looked at
them what she was thinking: *I'm okay.* It was Dylan
who broke the silence, leaning forward where he sat
and saying what no one else could.

"Let's not turn this into something it's not. We're in

QUAKE ◄ ◄ ◄

the middle of something bigger than any one of us can handle alone. We're going to need each other. We all have Meredith in common for one reason or another, and we all know she was a complicated person. But she loved every one of us in her own way. And she did what she had to do in a difficult time. We've all had to do the same, me included."

Dylan looked at Faith with some regret, thinking of how he'd brought her into this mess without asking her, but she took his hand without the slightest hesitation. This gave him the courage to go on. "And I'm very happy to discover I have a little sister."

Jade turned to Dylan and brightened. She had already been looking up to him as if he was her big brother. The fact that it had turned out to be true was beyond anything she could have imagined when Dylan had appeared on the mountain.

"You understand we don't have the same dad, right?" Dylan asked. "Mine's dead. Yours is right there."

Jade had always thought of Carl as her dad; that had not changed. But she didn't take her eyes off Dylan, not yet. The reality of having a big brother, especially one who loomed as large in the world as Dylan, was something to ponder. She seemed to be quietly thinking about a lot as her expression began to darken.

"How about we listen to the rest of the recording," Faith said as she saw Jade questioning everything she'd

67 ◄ ◄ ◄

ever known. "This is going to sort itself out, right? We're a family. We're in this together. Let's try to focus on the positive."

Jade stood up and glanced at the faces around the room. She finally looked at Clooger and seemed to fully calculate the information she'd just been given.

This is my dad.

My mom is dead.

Carl is my uncle.

Dylan is my brother.

Her expression had turned utterly blank, but the wheels were turning inside her head. It was too much, too fast.

"How can I trust any of you when you've misled me this whole time?"

And then Jade walked out of the room. She turned back at the last second and yelled, "I've got secrets of my own!"

Faith could hardly blame Jade. She knew what a break in trust felt like, but this was bigger than that. Jade didn't know who she was any longer. How could she?

"That could have gone better," Carl said.

Clooger didn't reply. He'd never been one for jokes to lighten a heavy load.

"Hawk, please," Faith said pleadingly. "Just play the rest of the message."

She hoped what remained wasn't full of more

surprises that didn't serve any purpose but to drive a wedge through an already fragile team.

Hawk was looking in the direction of where Jade had gone, his heart pulling him to places Faith couldn't afford to have him go. She needed his game-on best. Faith got up and tapped the screen herself, bringing Meredith back to life one last time.

I give you two more secrets now, ones that may help you finish what we have started.

The first is a fact known only to a few: Hotspur Chance has a plan. It's the plan that put him in the highest-security prison when it was discovered by officials in the State system. Hotspur never intended the States to grow so large so fast; he saw them instead as a method by which to radically alter the population of the world. Had he succeeded, he would have forever been known as the most successful mass murderer in the history of the world: a hundred million people, gone in a flash. The population of the United States cut in half in the blink of an eye.

Dylan motioned for Hawk to pause. He almost couldn't bring himself to say the words everyone was thinking, and he was glad Jade wasn't there to hear them.

"He developed the States to corral human population into small spaces," Dylan said. "So he could annihilate half of them."

"Beyond twisted," Hawk said. "Why would anyone want to do something like that, even if they could figure it out?"

Clooger answered, "Every generation has someone like Hotspur Chance. Hitler's methods weren't so different: he isolated a certain kind of person—"

"The Jews," Faith said. She had liked history more than any other subject in school.

"Yes, the Jews." Clooger nodded. "Hitler isolated them into central locations, then removed them from the population. He killed six million."

"And Stalin killed at least twenty million people," Faith remembered.

"But *why*?" Hawk asked again. No amount of logic, even at the level of an Intel, could properly answer the question for a fifteen-year-old kid. "Why would anyone do that?"

No one tried to answer Hawk, so the question hung in the air like a noose from a tree.

"It's efficient. It's contained. It's precise," Carl said out of nowhere.

Clooger nodded his agreement. "We know Hotspur was convinced that the only answer to saving the planet was to dramatically reduce the population."

"Wait, I never heard that," Dylan broke in. He was leaning forward, concern on his face, as if once again facts had been kept from him.

"We have always known this," Clooger said. "It's why he was Prisoner One, the deadliest man alive. Hotspur Chance envisioned the State system for two reasons: the reason everyone talks about, and the reason *no* one talks about. Yes, he designed the States to empty out vast amounts of space, that's true. But he also felt, very strongly, that the only way to save the planet was to remove large numbers of people quickly. Hundreds of millions."

"He was smart enough to create the blueprints for the States," Dylan said, catching on. "So he would have been smart enough to blow one of them up at any point."

"And to think I actually admired the guy when I was a kid," Hawk said, disoriented by the scope of evil being explained. "What an a-hole."

"Play the rest," Faith said. "Maybe Meredith knows how to stop him."

Hawk tapped the screen and Meredith's voice returned.

Did you know it was Hotspur Chance himself who chose the locations for each of the two States? And that he was the architect of the power grids? These things drift into memory and seem not to matter, but they do matter. They matter very much. What if Hotspur had hidden, within the skeletal bones of the States themselves, a way in which to control them? What if he could turn the whole of a State into the equivalent of nearly half a billion electric chairs?

This was one of many ideas I heard in my years at the compound, but it was always addressed as a theory, a thing to be reviewed and explored as the size of the States increased. And more importantly, something so complex that only Hotspur himself would ever have been able to seriously turn it into a threat of any consequence.

Hawk, you might be able to access the State mainframes and get into the original power-grid schematics. Depends on whether you're as smart as I think you are.

If Hotspur Chance is free once more, then you may have an unforeseen advantage. Wars are lost by thinking the impossible won't happen.

He assumes no one could know where he has gone. But I know. I've known all along. I know because I heard him tell it to Gretchen so many years ago.

Hawk paused the recording and took a quick look around the room.

"Why are we stopping?" Carl asked.

"I just wanted you all to know before we keep going," Hawk answered. "There's only one way to access a Western State mainframe."

"How?" Dylan asked.

Hawk sighed.

"From the inside."

No one spoke as the meaning of what Hawk had said sunk in. If they were going to have a chance of understanding what Hotspur might be planning to do, they'd need to do it from the inside of the Western State.

"Let's cross that bridge when we come to it," Faith said. "Play the rest."

Hawk engaged the recording one last time.

If Hotspur Chance is serious about putting this plan into action, he will do it from a location with coordinates that match the passcode used to unlock this message. It's the location he spoke of years ago, when we were only a few souls in the desert. I've sent search parties over the years and found nothing of interest here, but if he's escaped, then I believe this is where he went.

I intentionally positioned the last safe house as close to this set of coordinates as I could while providing for Jade's safety. This may prove useful now.

I have no idea what the world looks like because I'm no longer in it. Only you will know whether this information is useful.

I did my best. I expect no less from you.

With love and affection from far, far away.

I am Meredith, checking out for the final time.

Hawk was already translating the passcode into a set of coordinates when the audio recording stopped.

"45.5.122.67 translates into 45.5 degrees north by 122.67 degrees west."

Hawk brought up the holographic 3-D map in the middle of the room and zoomed in on an abandoned city.

"Portland, Oregon," Hawk said. "The coordinates give us about a five-mile radius around a shipyard on the Willamette River."

"How far?" Faith asked.

Hawk did some fast computations, and the holographic map zoomed in farther still. An abandoned shipyard sat at the bottom of the very mountain they were all standing on.

"Fifty-seven miles from here, give or take," Hawk said.

"We can get the jump on them," Clooger said. "We know they're down in that general area. They don't know we're up here."

"But five miles of space," Carl said. "Hotspur is like a needle in a haystack. He could be hiding in any number of abandoned buildings or vacant ships."

The room went silent as everyone let the information sink in. Hotspur Chance, the most dangerous criminal mind in the world, might be so close they could reach out and grab him. And he wasn't even a second pulse. He was vulnerable if only they could discover his location.

"If Wade and Clara are this close to us, some of us are in real danger," Carl said, shooting a quick glance at Clooger. "Jade can't move things with her mind or fly away like you all can. She's just a kid. A *normal* kid."

"I can't do any of that, either," Hawk said. "No matter how many times Dylan tries to teach me. It's not in my DNA."

Dylan had been trying to bring a first pulse out in Hawk ever since they'd met, but it was no use. If people could move things with their minds, Dylan could coax the skill out of them. But if the latent skill wasn't there, it wasn't there. And in Hawk's case, like so many millions of other people, there was no thread to grab onto, no hidden talent to pick up cars and move them with the power of his mind.

"We both got the short end of the stick," Carl said. "I'm a zero pulse, too."

"It could be worse," Dylan said, slapping Hawk on

the back. "You've got the brains, Carl's got the brawn. You guys are fine."

"It's late," Clooger said. "Let's all get a good night's sleep and hit this new plan hard in the morning. I'll talk to Jade, get her calmed down."

"Good luck," Carl said. "She can be bullheaded sometimes."

"Just like her dad," Dylan said, and finally there was a glimmer of lightness in the room, a brief moment when everyone smiled softly.

As they were leaving, Clooger pulled Faith and Dylan aside.

"Remember what I told you two," Clooger said quietly. "No pulse activity. *None*. If Clara and Wade are within sixty miles of here, they might feel it."

Everyone filed out until only Faith remained. She turned toward another long hallway on the other side of the room that led to a stairway and circled back overhead on the second floor. There she saw a flit of movement in the shadows, heard the soft sound of a creaking floorboard. Faith realized something then that made her worry even more about a young girl prone to rash decisions.

The young girl with jade-colored eyes had been listening all along.

Chapter 5

The Sound of Silence

Faith sat up in bed, startled by a sound she thought she'd heard before. She was prone to serious disorientation in the first minute of wakefulness. The screaming sound was back, accompanied by sunlight shining through the old pane window on the far side of the room. The morning light was, as usual, blinding her.

"They can't be watching that movie again, can they?"

And so it was that she retrieved her bat with her mind and started for the door still thinking that the scream, which had now dissolved into a melee of other sounds, was from a scene in a movie being played three doors down.

A projectile of some size and weight crashed through her window, and this event finally brought Faith Daniels completely awake.

"What the hell?" she said.

She heard the screaming voice again, but now she placed it in its actual location outside the lodge.

"Leave me alone!" was followed by a shrieking sound that could be projected only by a girl of a certain age.

"Jade?" Faith said out loud. She wanted to take flight, leaving through the window where glass had just shattered into her room along with a rock the size of a brick, but she knew better.

No pulse activity. None, Clooger had said, and he was right. Way too risky.

She realized at that moment that even the semiconscious moving of the baseball bat, which she had done more than once, was something she should not be doing. She set the bat down, suddenly concerned about her own behavior, and fled for the door. As she ran down the hall and up a narrow flight of stairs she yelled for Dylan and Clooger and Hawk, but no one answered.

"*What* is going on around here?" she said aloud as she reached the top of the stairs, crossed the lobby, and threw open the doors to the outside world.

What she found there turned her blood ice-cold.

"I told you I had a secret of my own!" Jade yelled at the top of her lungs.

Dylan, Clooger, and Carl were all standing in a circle around her, none of them any closer than twenty feet.

"Jade, stop doing this!" Clooger yelled. "You have to stop!"

"Oh, sure thing, *Dad*, whatever you say," Jade shot back.

Faith watched as Jade moved her arm swiftly up and a rusted-out snowplow lifted off the ground with shocking speed. It flew skyward a hundred feet in the span of two seconds, turned a sharp right, and went flying into the side of what had once been a ski run.

"Jade, no!" Faith screamed. "You can't be doing this!"

Jade screamed again. She put everything she had into that scream, bending over and letting it rip in a fit of primal anger Faith understood all too well. Faith had never really been a screamer, but she knew how this girl felt: angry, out of control, manipulated, imprisoned.

As Jade screamed, all manner of objects lifted off the ground and began flying through the air so fast that Carl and Clooger had to take shelter behind a boulder the size of a small house. An entire section of ski-lift chairs and the cables and poles that held them aloft pulled out of the earth like so many toothpicks. The tangled mess flew skyward, a rat's nest of metal that echoed down the mountain. Faith could tell Jade didn't have a clue how to control her pulse—a pulse she'd kept secret from everyone, including Carl. The tangle of wires and chairs and poles fell toward the earth in the direction of Clooger and Carl. That was when Faith and Dylan looked at each other and realized they'd have to intervene. Neither Carl nor Clooger had a second pulse, and Jade had lost all control. But Dylan and Faith were discovering, more and more, that when they worked together they were even more powerful.

Dylan picked up the house-sized boulder Clooger and Carl were hiding behind and hurled it into the air with his mind. Fifty feet overhead it smashed into one of the cables and the flying ski lift wrapped around rock like an octopus, the whole mess flying over the lodge and down the side of the mountain in a tangled, earsplitting knot of stone and cable and metal.

Faith moved in quickly, wrapping her arms around Jade and holding her in a bear hug. She lifted off the ground, carrying them both to the roof of the lodge before setting her back down. She could feel everything Dylan was doing, as if they were somehow connected. She looked skyward, saw Dylan there, and thought: *This is new. Something different is happening to us. Something bigger.*

But Jade was crying softly, all the steam gone out of her rage, and now was not the time to explore hidden new talents. "Are you finished or should I expect more stuff to start flying around?" Faith asked.

Jade wouldn't answer, so Faith took a deep breath, calmed her nerves, and tried to lighten up.

"Look, I understand you're angry, okay? But this power you've got and didn't tell anyone about is *dangerous*. Do you understand that? You could have hurt yourself."

"I know how to control it," Jade said, wiping away tears.

Faith wanted to say, *Oh, really? And did you know other people can feel a pulse that big? Did it cross your mind we might be detected?* But she knew that was the wrong way to help Jade.

"This is going to take some practice to master, and we're going to need to be very careful. I had a lot of trouble with my pulse when I first started using it. I was all over the place."

"I don't care," Jade said, softer and sadder than Faith had expected.

Poor kid, Faith thought. She put an arm around Jade and pulled her in close.

"No one is going to come up here, and we're not going down until you're ready," Faith consoled. "Just take it easy. Breathe."

Jade sucked in a big breath and finally looked at Faith, but by that time Faith was looking to the sky, making sure it was clear of something far worse than Jade could possibly imagine.

"I'm confused," Jade said.

"I know," said Faith. She pushed the loose hairs away from Jade's face and looked into her puffy, tear-stained eyes. "This power you have, how long have you known about it?"

Jade shrugged her usual shrug and looked down at her shoes. "A while, I guess."

"Does Carl know?" Faith asked. She couldn't imagine that he did, or he would have said.

Jade shook her head. "I didn't tell him. I guess I wanted something all to myself. I don't know. I don't know anything anymore."

"Parents are complicated," Faith said. "Especially when the world is messed up. My parents left me, too. Did you know that?"

Jade looked at Faith as if she was crazy.

"You think this is about *that*?" Jade said, exasperated. She looked out into the open space below, as if she was about to start throwing objects with her mind again.

"Whoa, hold on," Faith said. "What's gotten into you?"

Jade shook with frustration and pounded the side of a fist into the roof. She looked at Faith, laughing sadly.

"I know Carl loves me, and Clooger's fine. Two

dads, and they're brothers—it's weird, but it's fine. I'll survive. I'm practically grown-up anyway."

Faith's heart broke at the thought of such a young girl, just thirteen, being forced to become an adult in the crazy world she'd been born into.

"It's Hawk," Jade said. Her voice changed. She was almost happy. "We went for a walk last night under the moonlight. He held my hand and told me all about the real library you took him to. He was so nervous. He said you were a hand-holder. He likes hand-holding. And then he kissed me. He was shaking a little. It was adorable. And now this!"

Faith couldn't believe her ears. Jade had put the entire team at risk because of a crush? And yet she knew how powerful those feelings could be, how they could completely undo everything you thought you knew.

"He's a great guy," Faith said. "And smart, too. Obviously. And he likes you, I can tell. What's the problem?"

Jade's expression changed. She was confused.

"Don't tell me you don't know. Of course you know."

"Know what?"

Jade's face changed once more. This time her eyes widened at the thought of something Faith couldn't put together until Jade said the words.

"He's gone. Hawk took the HumGee down the mountain. He said he had to go do something no one else could do. He said he had to do it alone."

The tears started flowing again and Jade's lip quivered. "He wouldn't take me with him, but he said he'd come back for me. That's. Not. Possible! Once you go in you never come out. He's gone and he's never coming back."

"No way," Faith said as she pressed her hands flat against the top of the lodge, a sudden catlike alertness flowing through every vein.

"I know, right?" Jade said. "I'm never going to see him again."

But Faith wasn't reacting to the news about Hawk, though it was shocking and difficult to believe. She was reacting to something else.

"What is that?" Jade asked as she followed the direction of Faith's stare and tried to stand. Faith held her down by the arm and wouldn't let her go.

Two figures were coming in fast, flying toward the lodge, low against the tree line.

They had been found, again.

Faith turned to Jade and held her by the shoulders. She held her gaze, hard and fast.

"This is not your fault—don't you ever forget that. Do you understand?"

Jade saw the fear in Faith's eyes. Her nod was fast and nervous. Tears pooled in her bright green eyes as she began to process what she'd done.

"Listen to me," Faith said. Time was short, but this

was gut-wrenchingly personal. She knew exactly how Jade felt. "You didn't ask for the pulse. You didn't choose when to get born. You didn't decide to live up here. And you didn't choose who to fall in love with. None of this is your fault. Tell me you understand."

Jade nodded.

"Tell me!" Faith said, her full attention squarely on Jade as Wade and Clara Quinn flew closer to the lodge.

"It's not my fault," Jade said in a quiet, shaky voice.

That broke the spell and Faith was up in a flash, pulling Jade to her feet and looking to the sky.

"Get down the mountain at least a mile," Faith said in her serious voice. It was not a voice that was easy to disobey. "Hide in the woods and don't come out no matter what."

Jade nodded, dove into the air, and flew across the open space before the lodge, landing in a thicket of trees. Faith watched as Jade ran and ran, out of her line of sight.

There was no reason for Faith to hide her pulse anymore. She jumped off the roof and landed thirty feet below, where Dylan was still unaware of the approaching threat.

"They're coming," Faith said. She moved into Dylan's line of sight, holding his forearms. "Both of them."

Faith felt Dylan's muscles tighten in her hands and watched his expression change as he tried to turn his eyes to the sky. But she took his chin in her hand and pulled his attention back.

"This is going to be rougher than the last time. I can feel their rage."

Faith pulled Dylan into a kiss and held his face in her hands. When they parted she was close to tears.

"I love you," Dylan said. "And we're all going to get through this."

"Hawk's gone," Faith added, breathing in deep through her nose, forcing herself to be strong.

Dylan looked at Faith, a bewildered expression on his face. But then he recalibrated—game on, ready to roll. "One less person for them to kill. Let's make them sorry they came up here."

"You know it," Faith said, cracking her neck back and forth and feeling the side where a titanium dart had pierced her second pulse. She thought of the gun she'd taken from Clara and realized Clara would probably have another one with a chamber full of titanium bullets. Her invincibility was in serious question. But weapons were something that could be disengaged from the person holding them, which was a small bright spot.

"Job one in this thing is getting their weapons if they have any," Faith said. "We need to hit them hard with all we've got right from the start."

"We got company?" Clooger asked as he and Carl both stepped closer and sensed trouble.

"Wade and Clara are coming in hot," Faith said. "I'd say we've got twenty seconds, tops."

"Where's Jade?" the brothers asked over the top of each other.

"She's hiding in the woods, that way," Faith said, pointing off to her left where Jade had flown. "I used my severe voice and I told her to stay hidden. She will."

Clooger nodded tersely. "Game on."

Carl flexed his incredible arms, cracking his knuckles against one another, and nodded. "Let's give these two some fight."

"Fire on all cylinders," Dylan said. "You can't kill them but you can knock them around. And aim for any weapons either of them might be holding. That's the biggest thing you can do for us. If they're carrying weapons at all, they're loaded with the one thing that can hurt Faith."

"Roger that," Clooger said. He understood the threat facing Faith.

Carl and Clooger headed for the highest part of the lodge, a circular room not unlike a guard tower at a prison. Carl called it the bird's nest, and it was filled with weaponry collected over the years. Carl was a sharpshooter, a sniper of deer and elk, and he was possibly the most important player in the fight about to take place. He could even the playing field with the right shot. He was the one person who could disarm

Clara or Wade with a perfectly placed bullet.

"Let's do this," Dylan said, nodding to Faith as he touched her once more on the arm.

"I love you, too," she said, her voice trembling at the memory of being alone with him in the safe house, their arms around each other, such a brief moment outside time. Would she still linger on such things if the world ever calmed down and they could lie together in peace whenever they wanted? She didn't know. She didn't think she'd ever get the chance to answer the question.

Dylan and Faith flew apart, taking up stations on either side of the lodge as a chunk of earth the size of a double-wide trailer lifted out of the ground in front of Clara and Wade.

"Okay, now I'm worried," Faith said as she looked in every direction searching for what she would be able to pick up and use as weapons: two snowplows, a lot of rocks and boulders, some small outbuildings, trees if she could get them out of the ground. Not as much as she'd hoped for.

"Incoming!" Dylan said as he started hurling boulders at the approaching chunk of earth.

Faith did the same, picking up a snowplow and the tangled mess of wires and pylons left behind from Jade's tirade. The sky exploded with falling debris as Dylan went airborne, heading dead-on for the enemy.

Faith wanted more than anything to get out into the fray, but it was too risky until she was sure neither Wade nor Clara Quinn had a titanium-shooting weapon. She moved with lightning speed around the back of the lodge and flew like a low-flying rocket until she reached the other side. Then she drifted slowly up to the level of the roof and observed.

Faith could see the bird's nest on the farthest corner of the building, where Carl and Clooger were hunkered down low enough so Clara and Wade couldn't see them. Carl was training a rifle with a gigantic scope in Clara's direction. Dylan was in the middle of an air battle, throwing everything he could wrap his mind around.

"This isn't much of a welcome party," Clara said. She and Wade were right over the top of the lodge now, about thirty feet overhead. "I thought you'd be happy to see us."

"Come on. You must have been expecting our arrival," Wade added. "Even I don't think you're stupid enough to give away your position without having some surprises for us."

A rock the size of a baseball hit Wade in the back of the head and he lurched forward. When his eyes came back up, all pretense of humor was gone. He glared at Dylan with the face of a young man who came to kill.

"Hitting me from behind," Wade said. "I thought you had more character than that, Dylan. Actually, I take that back. You're a low-life drifter, just like your mom was."

But it hadn't been Dylan who'd sent the rock flying. Faith peered into the woods behind Wade and saw Jade standing there.

Faith shook her head, her hands pumping into fists. She wanted to get into the fight in the worst way, but she could see that Clara was packing two silver Lugers this time, not one. One was strapped to her leg; the other was in her hand. Faith touched her side, where the titanium bullet had pierced her second pulse, and remembered what it had felt like.

"Come on, Carl," Faith whispered pleadingly. "Fire before she gets moving."

She looked to where Clooger and Carl were hiding and saw the gun fire two times in succession. When she looked back at Clara, the gun that had been in her hand had been blown free.

"Time to move," Faith said. Her blood pressure shot up and she left her hiding place in the flash of an instant, cutting the space between herself and Clara in half before Clara could turn in Faith's direction. Clara reached for the second gun just as Faith slammed into her, sending them both end over end toward the ground. They hit and the second gun burst out of its holster. As they rolled and tumbled, Clooger picked up the two guns with his mind, moved them through the air, and hid them out of sight in the bird's nest. It all happened incredibly fast—a few seconds at most.

"What do we have here?" Wade said, staring at the bird's nest with a prowling, catlike smile on his face. A chunk of metal from a snowplow that had been ripped apart slammed into Wade's head and he reeled back. But this was Wade Quinn. He was a second pulse; he could take it. The only thing that could end Wade Quinn was a barrage of things that grew out of the earth. Dylan uprooted a fir tree, which took a lot out of him because the root systems were so tangled and difficult to rip out of the ground. He threw the tree like an arrow, bringing it down on Wade as he approached the duck blind, bullets flying.

Wade slammed into the ground, but seconds later the tree burst into the air, blowing a hole into the side of the lodge.

Faith had Clara momentarily pinned to a tree with her hand around Clara's neck. Two deep scars ran from Clara's forehead all the way down her left cheek and beyond her chin.

"See what you did to me?" Clara said as her voice shook with a weird laughter. Faith had stolen Clara's astounding beauty, driving two long gashes into her face that would always leave scars.

"My pleasure," Faith said. She saw a flit of movement behind her in the trees and knew Jade was close by, hiding in the trees. *Dammit, Jade. Run!* she thought.

Clara flew into the sky overhead, dragging Faith along when she wouldn't let go.

"You know how I hate all these trees," Clara said. "But I hate you even more."

Clara punched her knee upward and simultaneously brought an elbow across the side of Faith's head. Faith careened head over heels in the air and Clara kept pushing with her mind, making Faith gain more speed until she reached the roof of the lodge and hit back-first. The roof caved in and Faith found herself lying on the floor of the lodge staring up into a shaft of light.

She was up in a flash, back into the sky. But in that few seconds the tide had turned against her. Clara and Wade were hovering in front of the bird's nest, staring at easy prey as bullets bounced off their chests and faces.

"Why do they always think bullets are going to do anything?" Clara asked.

"You'd think they'd learn," Wade agreed.

"Leave them alone!" Faith screamed.

Dylan was uprooting two trees, putting everything he had into it, as Faith picked up everything that wasn't nailed down and sent it all in a maelstrom up into the air, dropping it all on top of Wade and Clara.

They stayed under the pile of rubble for no more

than a few seconds, then burst free and shook like two dogs jumping out of a bathtub.

Dylan had the trees uprooted and moved fast toward the milieu as Wade turned calmly toward the duck blind. Faith couldn't see his face, but she was sure he was smiling.

"Don't do it, Wade! You can take me!" Faith screamed.

Wade didn't turn, but Clara did. She stared at Faith for a long beat.

"Payback time."

Wade's hand flitted ever so slightly, and Carl rose out of the blind. He kept firing, growling under all that muscle and gritting his white teeth. The gun he was holding was suddenly ripped from his hands. It turned in his direction in midair.

"Wade, no!" Clooger tried to fly directly into Wade, but Wade set the gun to firing before Clooger could cut the distance between them. A barrage of bullets sprayed the air back and forth, tearing through Carl and Clooger. Their chests burst with blood as they shook in the air.

When the firing stopped, both men fell to the ground and the two brothers stared at each other, surprised beyond words that death had finally cornered them.

Faith was in a total state of shock as Dylan turned

the trees roots-first and pounded them down on top of Wade and Clara. He held them under fresh, live roots, twisting the trees in a circle and boring them into the earth.

"Faith, you need to help me!" Dylan said. "I can't hold them both down by myself." Faith shook her head and put the power of her mind to work on the task at hand: snuff the life out of the monster that had just gunned down Carl and Clooger in cold blood.

She watched as the trees swirled, tangling around Clara and Wade, their heads rolling around in dirt as they spun and spun under the weight of one of the few things that could destroy them both. Faith looked across at Dylan and reached in his direction without thinking. The intensity of what was happening all around her fell into the background as she felt the force of her feelings for him. Faith felt an immense power building inside her, not from the hate she felt for these two demons, but from what she shared with Dylan. She felt the mountain moving underneath her, a quake of activity.

Did I make that happen?

She looked up at the ragged peak and thought she saw pieces of rock breaking free.

Wade let fly his own powers and the trees that were piled on top of him stopped, rising slowly and then slamming back down in front of him. Faith shook her head and refocused. They were at a standstill when Wade spoke.

"Let us go and we won't kill the girl," Wade said.

Jade had come running out of the forest, and now she was kneeling over Carl and Clooger, sobbing and trying to hold back the flow of blood from both men.

"I'm sorry," Jade kept saying. And in their dying breaths, both Carl and Clooger kept repeating the same words: *Run, run, run!*

"Let them go," Faith said, but Dylan kept pushing. "Please, Dylan. Let them go! We can't let them kill Jade, too."

Dylan let up just enough to give Wade and Clara the chance they needed. With incredible speed the trees were blown away and the two of them were gone, like a flash of lightning, off and away from the lodge. At the same moment they picked up everything but the lodge itself, filling the sky with a tornado of objects big and small that trailed behind them for a hundred yards.

When the dust cleared, it wasn't just Wade and Clara who were gone.

Jade was gone, too.

They'd kept their promise not to kill her, but that didn't mean they couldn't take her as a bargaining chip.

Faith and Dylan knelt down next to Clooger and Carl. Both men were barely holding on to their last breaths.

Carl lifted his massive arm and grabbed Dylan's shirt, pulling him close. He spoke in a garbled whisper.

"You gotta get her back, D. Don't fail me on this one."

"If it's the last thing we do," Dylan said as he looked at all the bullet marks in Carl's shirt. There was no plugging all the holes that were pumping blood into the dirt. "We'll get her back."

Clooger was smiling as he gazed up at Faith. He wasn't aware that Jade was gone, and it was better that way.

"Carl's wrong," Clooger said, coughing up a crimson stain of blood. "War doesn't have to go on forever. You can end this thing, Faith. You can do it."

Faith nodded as she cried and held Clooger's head in her hands. She didn't know if she believed him, but she knew she was going to try. Both men died at the same time, in what would later be remembered as the Timberline Massacre. But they didn't die before looking at each other one last time.

"You did good, brother," Clooger said. "You raised her right."

"You too, Cloog. You're a hell of a fighter."

They drifted into the great unknown, leaving Dylan and Faith to figure out what to do next all by themselves.

"I felt the earth move," Dylan said as he looked at

Faith, confused and heartbroken. "Could they be that powerful? Could they move something that big?"

"I don't think it was them," Faith said through her tears. "I think it was us."

A deep silence covered the grounds of the lodge and the clouds rolled in as Faith and Dylan fell into each other's arms, exhausted and emotionally destroyed.

Chapter 6

Airwalk at Stalefish

Faith was sitting on a pinewood porch swing enveloped in an old familiar feeling, thinking about how fast things had come unglued. She had arrived at a lodge on top of a mountain to find a few weeks of peace, to rest her weary bones and tender emotions. She had let herself feel calm, happy even.

And here she sat, everything in her life blown apart all over again.

Hawk was gone, unprotected, without a sound ring. He was totally on his own, rogue, making choices that could get him killed. For all Faith knew, he was already dead. She shook her head at the thought of it. A world without Hawk in it didn't seem possible. The world needed people like Hawk, people with optimism and energy who could wipe away the darkness just by walking into a room.

Clooger and Carl were dead, the only card-carrying adults they had, gone in a few seconds of gunfire. It reminded her that life was a delicate situation for most people. They could go at any moment, cut short by an approaching bus or a knife-wielding madman. It had become all too easy for Faith to think as if she and everyone else close to her were immortals, or damn close.

What she really wanted was a tattoo; the sting of a needle to numb the pain. A tattoo so big it would cover her entire body and make her forget that Clooger was gone. Carl she'd barely known, but Clooger? The heaviness of his loss felt as if it had enough weight to crush her bones into dust. She could think of it for only a second or two at a time without feeling her chest fill with a sob that would last forever. She had to back away from the information, fill her mind with better memories. The problem was how many bad memories already existed inside her, stacked like cordwood, safely locked away beyond feeling. Faith was starting to feel as if she might burst into flames at any moment, every searing memory rushing forward at once.

Even though Clooger had been a single pulse, unable to protect himself from bullets or bombs or anything else, she'd still seen him as more than just a partner; he was their leader. He had experience Faith didn't have and a wellspring of courage she sometimes lacked. Clooger and Dylan—these two had her back and the power to help her destroy whatever evil approached. And now one of them was gone.

I'm sorry, Clooger, she thought as she looked through the trees and felt the tears pooling. *Sorry we couldn't get you on the other side of this thing before it was too late.*

She looked up at the top of the mountain, the peak that so intrigued her, and thought about how she'd made the whole mountain shake under her feet. It scared her to think about so much power. Her thoughts turned to Jade just as Dylan stepped through the screen door and let it fall back on its rusted spring, clanging against the jamb. He sat down beside Faith and the porch swing wobbled forward.

"We should have known. How did we miss it?"

There was no doubt what he was referring to: Jade's power.

"I can understand why she chose to hide it," Faith admitted. She rocked back on the porch swing and stared out into the forest, her eyes narrowing against the light coming through the trees. "Everyone else was keeping secrets from her. I think she knew that. This was her secret. I just wish she'd have known how dangerous it was."

"As soon as we understood she was my half sister we should have all been like, 'So yeah, maybe she's got the pulse running through her veins. She's Meredith and Clooger's daughter.' They both had single pulses. It was possible Jade would be a carrier."

"But no one would have guessed she'd been secretly messing around with it. That's what I don't understand. To have that kind of power, she had to be at it awhile."

"Maybe not," Dylan said. He glanced around nervously. "Remember how I told you it took me some time to get my power under control?"

Faith nodded. She did remember.

"It was especially bad when I was angry. Meredith always said kids were the most unpredictable once they knew the power they had. I remember I didn't understand how dangerous it was. How people could get hurt."

"But how did she unlock it without help?" Faith asked. "You had to bring out my pulse. Hers just showed up out of nowhere?"

Dylan breathed a heavy sigh. He didn't want to say what might have been true, but he did.

"My mom used to disappear for weeks on end. No one knew where she went."

Faith started putting two and two together.

"You think she came up here."

Dylan shrugged. "If she did, she might have trained Jade in her sleep. Maybe they talked, maybe Jade didn't even know her mother was there. You didn't know I was outside your window all those months. You were asleep."

Faith thought about it a moment, her eyes narrowing as she tried to remember what it had been like moving an object with her mind for the first time. It had been a heady experience.

"Maybe my mom just wanted to make sure Jade could defend herself if trouble ever showed up on the mountain."

"But why wouldn't she have told Carl or Clooger?"

Dylan shook his head. He didn't seem to know.

"She's an orphan now, like us," Faith said, and that was enough to simmer down her feelings toward Jade and remind her that while they were all orphaned on the face of the earth, Jade was the youngest.

Faith turned to Dylan and saw that he was holding a letter in his hand. He looked at it, half smiling and shaking his head.

"It's from Hawk."

"Have you read it? I'm not sure how much more bad news I can take right now."

"I found it in his room, but I haven't opened it yet. I wanted us to hear it together."

Faith nodded, pulling her feet up on the porch swing and turning to face Dylan. She leaned her side onto the back of the swing, wrapping her arms around

her knees. It was as if she was preparing herself for a
body blow.

"Here goes," Dylan said. He tore open the envelope
and began reading.

> *I hope you read this before anyone came looking for
> me, because I'd hate to think anyone got hurt or our
> position was compromised because of me. Either way,
> chances are I was way too far gone before you started
> out, and I'm a tricky navigator. You have no idea which
> way I went and you're not going to know. Me and the
> HumGee are doing this alone. End of story. Also, sorry
> for taking the cool car, but I needed it.*
>
> *Everyone has a role to play here, and you heard
> what Meredith said. Mine is to figure out what
> Hotspur Chance built into the foundation of the power
> grid. No one else can do that but me, and I can do it
> only from inside one of the States. That information
> will be hard enough to get ahold of inside, but outside,
> it's a total nonstarter. Hopefully I can find Neal
> Gordon and he can help me, but I have a feeling this
> is going to require an Intel level of intelligence to figure
> out. Accessing a hidden layer of technology running
> under a city with hundreds of millions of people is a
> tall order. From a deductive-reasoning point of view, it
> was an easy problem to solve: I had to leave without
> telling you.*

"He's been watching too many action movies," Faith said.

"You might be right."

"What else does it say?"

Dylan continued:

We need a relay station. There's not one up there where you guys are now, but if you can get down into Portland without being detected, we can send messages back and forth from a relay station there. Take the Burnside Bridge over the river. Follow it until you get into the old downtown. Then look for the Koin Building. Can't miss it, shaped like a rocket and the angles look like they were made out of Legos. Go to apartment number 1106. That one used to belong to Paul Allen. That guy was a billionaire; he helped start Microsoft about a hundred years ago.

"I read about him in American Technical History," Faith said.

"Me too," Dylan said. "He owned pro sports teams and had a passion for Jimi Hendrix music."

Faith raised her eyebrows up and down: *Keep reading, Professor.*

Dylan read on:

One of Allen's obsessions before he died was classic computers and console games. He had some really rare stuff, including a 2018 model that used radio waves to send messages across any network. The product bombed, never made it out of beta. But Allen had three of them, since his company, Vulcan, helped fund the development. I'm betting he kept at least one on display in his apartment, and if we're lucky it's still there. It'll be a Tablet, black casing. Should have the solar powering built in, but it will be dead when you find it. Get it into the sunlight and we should be able to send messages back and forth without being traceable. Write this down:

Relay one: 342459

Relay two: PPd23ed (case sensitive)

Relay three: WS404.12.7.8

Enter those into the network settings. That should jump between three totally independent systems: radio waves, abandoned Wi-Fi, and Western State digital. If we use that pathway, no one will trace and we should be able to send and retrieve messages. Use the app mail resident on the device, log in as:

paulallen@itsme.com

password: if6was9

You'll get a message from me—airwalk@stalefish.ws

"Airwalk at Stalefish?" Faith asked. "What's gotten into him?"

Dylan offered a half smile, the most he could muster given the dire circumstances.

"He never told you about his Tony Hawk obsession?"

"No, he didn't."

"Must have been guy stuff. He named himself after Tony Hawk, that's how much he wished he could skateboard like this guy. Tony Hawk was this badass skateboarder before the equipment went all hovercraft in 2030. He invented the Airwalk and the Stalefish."

Faith didn't have any idea what Dylan was talking about.

"They're classic skateboarding tricks."

"And 'If 6 Was 9' is a Jimi Hendrix song," Faith said. She was more into classic rock than most. "How much more did he write?"

Dylan scanned the page. "Couple more paragraphs."

I can do this, you guys, but you have to trust me. And if this means I'm stuck in the Western State for the rest of my life, then that's what it means. People are giving up their lives for this shit. A madman is on the loose who wants to kill a few hundred million people in cold blood. This is worth it. And I know you two. You wouldn't have let me go or you'd be trying to keep tabs on me constantly or I'd be doing the same

to you. *We all need to focus on our part. You two*
are equipped to face Chance and Wade and Clara.
You can kick ass against them in a fight. I can do the
most good behind enemy lines, not in the line of fire. I
wouldn't last five minutes with those a-holes.

I left Jade a letter, too, telling her where I've gone.
She might have gotten it before you guys got this one.
If so, I'm really worried about her. I think I might
love her.

No, seriously.

Maybe when this is all over she'll come find me,
maybe not. I hope she does (P.S. Dylan, now I know
what you were talking about, i.e., Faith). Either way
I have a feeling she might try to come for me and get
lost in the woods, so I've tagged her with a tracking
device. It's old tech to keep it off the grid, so you need
to be within five miles of her location. But if she's gone
when you get this she couldn't have gotten that far. Just
use the old wifi protocols with the GPS setting on one
of your Tablets and search for Lucy Pevensie. If she's
gone, you'll find her.

How to close this thing out?

I'm going with 'See you soon' because 'I'm trapped
inside the Western State and we'll never breathe the
same air again' is too messed up.

I bet I'll figure a way out once we kick some ass.
Hawk

Faith and Dylan looked at each other in silence and understood they'd just been given an unintended gift.

"We can find Jade," Faith said.

Dylan realized something else, equally as important: "And if we can find Jade, we can find Hotspur Chance and the Quinns."

"He's right, you know," Faith said, standing as she stretched, arching her back like a cat waking from a dream. "We'd have tried to stop him. It's better this way. Sad, but better."

"If anyone can bust out of the Western State, it's Hawk," Dylan said as he folded up the letter and stuffed it back in the envelope. He stood and looked at Faith. There would always be something elusive about her, and it made him wonder whether he would ever completely win her heart. He hadn't been honest with her at the start, because at the time he'd seen Faith as Meredith had seen her: a weapon in an ongoing struggle. Nothing more, nothing less. He regretted letting himself feel so cold, especially now that he'd fallen in love.

Faith tucked her head under his chin.

"Don't pull away from me," Dylan said, feeling the warmth of her body. "Don't leave. I can't do this without you."

Faith knew this was not a request that had anything to do with Faith's physical presence. There had been times in the past when she stopped trusting anyone.

Times when she collapsed into herself and could not be found, even by Dylan.

"We need to bury them," Faith said, tears soaking into Dylan's black T-shirt. "And not with our minds. We need to put in the work this time. We need to feel the weight of a shovel in our hands."

"I was thinking the same thing," Dylan agreed, and for a moment he choked on the words. He was having just as a hard a time as Faith was. "It's impossible to imagine a world without Clooger in it, ya know?"

"Yeah, I know," Faith said.

And so they found the tools they needed in one of the sheds and searched until they discovered the perfect spot. It was a bluff that looked over the far side of the mountain, to places neither of them had ever been and might not ever go. The lodge loomed behind them as the bodies rose into the air and landed at their feet, Dylan's thoughts bringing them near.

The digging was hard work, just what Faith needed. She gritted her teeth and groaned with every stab of the earth until she was standing so far inside the hole she could barely see out. Sweat poured off her skin and down her face, mixing with the mud and the tears and the pain.

When they carefully moved the bodies into the double-wide burial space they'd made for Clooger and Carl, Faith vowed to leave her grief buried in the mountain until the real work was done.

"We're going to finish what you started," Faith said, the power in her voice returning as grief was being swept away, if only for a time. "And if it's the last thing we do, we're bringing Jade and Hawk back here. Count on it."

An eagle flew overhead, shrieking into the sun.

"You were good men in a hard time," Dylan said as he leaned hard on his shovel, catching his breath. Faith looked at Dylan, and she could tell he wanted to say more but couldn't. He closed his eyes and dropped his head. If there were tears they were his own, and Faith didn't try to stop them. She let the moment stand for what it was: a young man losing the closest thing he'd ever had to a father, with a long and difficult road still ahead.

They filled the hole they'd dug, a much faster task than making it, and stood before the soft earth with nothing left to do. The empty space with no task to complete hit Faith hard and her breath turned shallow. She swallowed back tears and stabbed the shovel into the ground, where it stood like a tombstone.

"So that's it, then," Faith said, her voice shaking with emotion. "They're gone. They're all gone. I'm running out of people Wade and Clara can take from me."

Dylan was stooped over with his hands on his knees and he looked up, the sun blinding him from behind

QUAKE ◄ ◄ ◄

Faith's head. What he saw there was a girl transformed. She was no longer the broken thing that had looked so beaten only an hour ago. The task had burned the sorrow out of her veins and the words she spoke were the last wisp of self-pity.

What remained was something Dylan had seen before, and he realized his mother had been right about Faith Daniels. When she was pushed too far, Faith knew how to push back like nobody else in the world.

"You ready?" she asked, her face awash with purpose and resolve as she wiped away a single tear.

"Yeah," Dylan said, standing as the sweat ran down his chest and arms. "I'm ready."

The force of Faith's and Dylan's will was about to carry them straight into the heart of the beast.

111 ◄ ◄ ◄

Chapter 7

Urban Cowboys

Faith and Dylan cleaned up and packed some basics in two packs: food, water, med kit, extra clothes. Faith went into Jade's room and found the entire collection of Narnia books, lined up in a row on a small shelf next to her bed. There had been seven books at one time, but now there were only six. Faith took the one on the far left—*The Magician's Nephew*—and stuffed it in her bag.

"Have you read them?" Dylan asked from the doorway where he stood.

Faith nodded yes, and they left the room together, walking down the hall toward the main entry.

"So you know about what order to read them in," Dylan said as they arrived in the main hall where their last meeting had taken place. The fireplace was empty of life now, a vacant mouth of ashes and soot. "*The Magician's Nephew* was written later than *The Lion, the Witch and the Wardrobe*, but chronologically, *The Magician's Nephew* comes first in the story."

"Yeah, I know that," Faith said, listening only sort of as she pushed open the door of the lodge and sun poured in. "But *The Lion, the Witch and the Wardrobe* still *feels* like the first one, don't you think?"

"I guess so," Dylan agreed. "Later on they moved it to the front, but when the books were first published about a hundred years ago, *The Magician's Nephew* was nearer to the end."

"You went through a Narnia phase, too?" Faith asked, happy that they'd found something new they had in common.

"I think I was ten," he said, a bashful smile on his face. "I was a little bit obsessed. I used to draw maps and imagine myself wandering around in Narnia, having these incredible adventures. And I loved the idea of talking to animals like they did. Couldn't get enough of it."

"You know what would make a very nice tattoo?" Faith thought out loud. "That lamppost inside the forest, standing all alone, and under that, those famous C. S. Lewis words: *Courage, Dear Heart*."

"Sounds like a good one," Dylan agreed. "The

passcode Hawk gave us—Lucy Pevensie?"

"She's one of the main characters," Faith finished Dylan's thought.

Faith looked at her Tablet and set the name into the GPS settings. There was no return, as expected. Wade and Clara had taken Jade into the urban death trap of Portland, Oregon, down the far side of the mountain.

"Is Lucy alive at the end of the story?" Faith asked.

"Very much so," Dylan said.

Faith nodded, taking this as a cosmic literary sign that they might succeed in their effort to get Jade back, even as she worried otherwise.

"We're coming back here," Faith said as she glanced back at the battered lodge behind her. Windows were broken out, and there was a snowplow tilted on its side and rammed into one corner of the building. A boulder had punched a wide hole into the tilted roof. Though it had been damaged by a violent battle, the lodge still felt like a sacred place.

"Kind of lonely up here now, know what I mean?" Dylan asked in a hushed tone. He was listening to the sounds all around him—the birds and the wind in the trees—and feeling, deep down, how empty the place was.

"Yeah, I know what you mean," Faith said as she stared into a breeze and squinted her eyes. "It will feel right again when there are four of us."

"We can find them," Dylan said. "Let's make it as hard as we can for them to find us."

Any pulse activity had the risk of alerting Hotspur Chance, Wade, and Clara, especially since they were stationed in a hidden location so close to the mountain, so Faith and Dylan walked at a brisk pace, putting several miles behind them in under an hour. When they crossed a mountain stream they drained their water bottles and refilled, snacking on dried fruits and nuts.

"I miss home already," Faith said, looking back up the mountain.

"It did kind of feel like home, didn't it?" Dylan added. "It got under our skin quick. We'll make it back."

Faith kept thinking about the mountain peak with its sharp rocks and jagged spires, how it looked treacherous and striking.

"We should be able to cut the distance in half today and hopefully find the Koin Building by midday tomorrow," Dylan said as he wiped his brow and sucked in a deep hit of mountain air.

"Sounds about right," Faith agreed. She was feeling tired from all the digging and walking and emotional pummeling, but she didn't want Dylan to see it. She'd go as long as he did, no questions asked.

At nightfall they camped at the base of the mountain,

twenty-three miles behind them and a little more than that to go.

"Walking is overrated," Faith said as she checked the Lucy GPS setting once more and got no return.

"I don't know where you get your energy reserves," Dylan said, flopping down in the grass with his limbs splayed out in every direction. "I'm on empty. Wiped out. Stick a fork in me."

Faith sat down next to him and reclined with her head resting on his chest.

"You're a lousy pillow," Faith said, digging the side of her face into his shoulder. "Too much muscle, not enough fat."

Dylan was already breathing heavily.

"Are you asleep?" Faith asked. She didn't believe it until five seconds went by and Dylan didn't answer. "You're totally asleep."

Faith was still a bundle of nerves even after all the walking and digging she'd filled her day with. She sat up and rifled through her bag until her hand touched *The Magician's Nephew*. She took out the small paperback novel and held it at arm's length. The light was fading, but she might be able to get in a chapter. Maybe it would carry her away from the worries of the day and remind her of better times.

She reread awhile about two children, a girl named Polly and a boy called Digory, who live in two row houses with an adjoining wall. They decide to explore the attic attaching the two houses and accidentally enter a study, where they find Digory's uncle.

Faith read the part where Uncle Andrew persuades Polly to touch a magic yellow ring, sending her into a world beyond the forest. Digory would have to go into the world of Narnia and bring her back. There in the margin were some words, written in blue pen:

If I was Polly, Hawk would come and save me.

Jade had written in the margin, and this put a sad sort of smile on Faith's face as she heard a slight sound in the underbrush a few yards away. The sound was close—too close—and she glanced at Dylan. He was in a deep sleep, and who knew what he might do if he woke suddenly? Faith stayed very still and then it struck her that they'd made a mistake: *We didn't bring any conventional weapons.*

It hadn't even crossed their minds to bring a gun or a knife or even a baseball bat, because they hadn't needed weapons to protect themselves for a long time. They were human weapons, but without being able to use their pulses, their powers were limited.

The sound inched another step closer in the gloom of the forest at the bottom of the mountain.

Faith set the book down and quietly stood up. As she did so, a bear came into view, rocking as it walked under its massive weight.

"Dylan," Faith said, kicking him in the side with just enough force for him to understand he had better wake up.

"What is it?" he said, groggy and half out of it as he sat up and wiped a hand across his face.

The bear moved closer and Faith thought about everything she'd been through. She could stay still and let the bear have its moment, show its dominance. But something had been quietly gnawing at her for hours and she thought this bear might be able to help her, so she moved toward the bear.

"Hey, whoa," Dylan said, up on his feet in an instant and reaching out for Faith. "Let it pass. She'll move off if we're not a threat."

Two cubs peeked out from behind the mother and Dylan changed his tune.

"Get your bag, Faith. We need to move."

But Faith kept walking, steady and deliberate, until she stood within five feet of a thousand-pound animal with claws designed to rip things in two.

The grizzly stood, towering over Faith by several feet, and growled so low and loud it shook Faith's bones.

"Turn around," Faith said. "Go back up the mountain where you came from."

The bear slapped Faith across the face, its claws ripping along her cheek and across her nose. The blow snapped Faith's head hard to the left. It should have broken her neck, torn her face into shreds of flesh, but she turned back to the bear unharmed. Her second pulse was way too strong for a beast of this size.

The bear fell forward and pushed Faith to the ground, leveling all its weight onto her body. Its face drew within an inch of Faith's and it roared. She felt the power of an incredible animal as it rocked her with blow after blow to the face. Faith had to be careful not to let too much in. Just a sliver, that's all she needed. If the protection of her second pulse was measured in many miles, then she pulled the protective barrier it created back by an inch. She felt the last blow, felt her brain fire with pain, felt the claw as it sliced across her skin. She wondered what it had felt like for Carl and Clooger as the bullets pierced their skin. And she understood in a very small way what it must have been like to know their lives were coming to an end.

"You can't really hurt me," Faith said, putting the full force of her second pulse back into play. "I kind of wish you could. But you can't."

The bear stepped back and looked at her cubs, suddenly afraid of this unkillable thing it had encountered. Faith stood up and touched her face, but found no blood there.

"What are you doing, Faith?" Dylan asked as he came alongside her. The bear and its cubs moved away, deeper into the forest.

"Sometimes I need to experience a little pain in order to feel human again," Faith said, putting an arm around Dylan's side. "I'm fine. Let's get some sleep."

They lay in a spoon, Dylan's arm wrapped around her, and she thought of the bear wandering off into the woods. She also thought of the yellow ring and where Polly had gone off to. As she finally fell asleep she felt sure that Polly and the bear had ended up in the same place, somewhere outside the wrecked world Faith had endured every day of her life.

The next morning as they walked farther away from the base of the mountain and nearer the urban sprawl of a fallen city, Faith kept looking over her shoulder, searching for the bear. But she never saw it again, and as they approached what was left of downtown Portland, she knew she never would.

"Looks like all the bridges are out but that one," Dylan said, squinting into the morning sun. A wide river stood between them and the hollowed-out downtown, huddled tight against the opposite side. Several bridges had once spanned the distance, but only one was intact now.

"GPS says it's the Burnside Bridge," Faith said, touching the screen to move the map from side to side. She pointed to a pinkish-colored building directly across the river. "That's the Koin Building."

"Still no sign of Jade?" Dylan asked as he knelt down and tied his boot.

"I'm a little surprised," Faith said, shaking her head. "I really thought they'd be here."

Portland was more than five miles across, but not by much. Either Hotspur Chance had decided the city was too risky and moved somewhere else, or he'd never been here to begin with. Either way it was probably some very bad news.

"Let's get to the Koin Building and see if Hawk can help," Dylan said. "We could fly over, swim, or take the bridge. What's your poison?"

Faith smiled because she knew they couldn't fly over the river without the risk of being detected, and swimming just seemed like a lot of work that would leave them cold and wet.

"Bridge," they both said at once.

Dylan put an arm around Faith. "Great minds think alike."

They reached the span twenty minutes later and found a slew of abandoned cars and buildings. Faith hated zeroed cities. They always seemed like zombie towns, at once sad and scary as hell. The bridge angled up gradually, cracked and strewn with old bicycles and pickup trucks and taxi cabs.

"It's as if this stuff was put here on purpose," Dylan said, noticing that some of the vehicles were turned up on their sides, creating a pathway of rubble they needed to crisscross through in order to pass. "Something doesn't feel right."

Faith felt the same way as they continued on, finding more and more cars with blown-out windows filling the bridge. The pathway through narrowed even more until they reached the midpoint of the bridge and an opening appeared, encircled by abandoned cars.

"This is getting weird," Faith said.

Steel beams rose into the sky overhead, where a makeshift fort had been built out of plywood and random junk. A bullhorn sounded from somewhere inside the structure.

"How about you two hold up right there so I can get a good look at you."

The voice had a cowboy drawl to it, as if whoever was up there staring down at them was fresh off the rodeo circuit.

"We're not looking for trouble," Dylan said, putting his hands out to his sides to show that he was not carrying anything. "We're unarmed, just passing through."

There was no reply, but all the windows in the cars that circled Faith and Dylan unexpectedly filled with shotgun barrels.

"It's like the O.K. Corral," Faith said, drawing on some long-ago history lecture she'd sat through when she was ten or eleven. "They've even got cowboy hats."

QUAKE ◀ ◀ ◀

"What's the O.K. Corral?" Dylan asked curiously.

"Didn't you *ever* study?"

"Of course I did. I know a lot of stuff. But I read a lot of comic books in history class." Dylan shrugged.

Faith thought of how easy it had become to rely on the fact that the guns trained on them would have no effect, even if they all fired at once and every single one of them hit its target. "Hang on now," the voice overhead said into the bullhorn. "I'm comin' down to check this out."

Dylan rolled his eyes. "Should we just leave? Let them shoot?"

Faith thought that was a terrible idea and shook her head. *Chill. Let's let this play out.*

Faith glanced around the circle and saw that every head in every window was covered with a cowboy hat. They were some sort of urban gang of gun-loving wackos who'd never gone into the States and chosen instead to take over what was left of Portland as an outpost. Faith and Dylan had tried to cross a checkpoint of some kind.

"This just gets weirder," Dylan said as he looked up into the beams of steel. The whole fort was moving down on cables like an outdoor junk elevator. It stopped on the pavement of the bridge and a metal door swung open.

A bearded man with a plaid shirt, cowboy boots,

123 ◀ ◀ ◀

and a ten-gallon hat walked out onto the bridge. When he entered the circle of cars Dylan and Faith stood inside of, he motioned for everyone to settle down.

"Let's have a look at what we got here," the man said warily. He was packing a pistol in a holster and holding an assault weapon that looked as if it could fire a thousand rounds a minute.

"Like I said," Dylan offered, hands out at his sides, "we're not looking for trouble. We just want to pass through."

The man's eyes narrowed and he stepped closer to Dylan. He ran his free hand over a gray mustache that looked as if it hadn't been trimmed for about a decade.

"Name's Clay, how about you two?" the man said. He appeared to be chewing on a small bit of gum or his lip or something left over from breakfast, it was hard to say which.

"We'd rather not say," Dylan answered, taking a step toward Clay and flexing his arms. Dylan could be an imposing figure. Cool confidence oozed off him in situations like this, which had a certain power of its own. It was a power Clay didn't seem to take much notice of.

"I generally prefer it when I know names before I start shooting, but it's your funeral either way."

Clay raised the assault rifle so it pointed at Dylan and laid his finger on the trigger.

"Go ahead," Dylan goaded, stepping into the barrel

of the gun until it touched his chest. "See what happens."

"Okay, you two," Faith said. "Enough testosterone already. I'm Faith, this is Dylan, and we're passing through. Is there some sort of toll or something? Because if there is you can check our packs. We're dead broke."

Clay didn't take his eyes off Dylan the entire time Faith spoke. He took a deep breath, and then he fired about twenty rounds into Dylan's chest, knocking Dylan onto the ground with the force of the bullets. The man turned the gun on Faith and fired a similar number of rounds, but Faith saw them coming and braced herself enough to stay standing when the bullets stopped flying.

Clay held his gun out to the side and someone exited a creaky car door, ran over and took the gun, and returned to where he'd come. Dylan didn't seem to know what to do, so he stayed on the ground and looked at Faith. *Now what?*

Clay surprised everyone and reached a hand down toward Dylan.

"You're as tough as your mom said you would be. And headstrong, just like her."

"Wait," Faith said as Dylan took Clay's hand and Clay pulled him up onto his feet. "You knew *Meredith*?"

"Knew?" Clay's attention turned dramatically toward Faith and no one else. "Whatcha mean, *knew*?"

Faith looked around and saw how out in the open they were, how exposed and dramatic it all must have looked, especially with the gunfire.

"You seem to know a lot more about us than we know about you," she said. "But I can promise you this: Portland might be your home, but it also feels like the most dangerous place on earth. Can we disband this little show and sit down somewhere less conspicuous?"

Clay looked around at the ridiculous spectacle he'd created and seemed to agree. He nodded to a woman in a wide-brimmed Stetson who sat in a late-model solar car that was pockmarked with bullet holes and dents.

"Saddle up!" the woman yelled, and all the cars moved in a line around the sides of the fort that had been lowered onto the bridge. They moved in silence, each of them running on some combination of solar and electrical power.

A few minutes later all three were in the fort, which had been lifted into the air above the bridge. Light streamed in through cracks in the corrugated-metal walls as Clay offered them each a chair at a table in the center of the room.

"Is she gone?" Clay asked solemnly. "Just tell me that much and we can start exchanging information freely."

"Yeah," Dylan said. "She's gone. A few weeks ago."

"I figured as much," Clay said, shaking his head.

"We got some intel on the crazy stuff going down in the Western State, but it was spotty. Figured she was involved in whatever the dustup was."

"It was a little more than a dustup," Dylan said.

He nodded, looked hard at Faith, then Dylan. "You do know you're public enemy number four and five, right?"

There was an ancient Tablet on the table, at least twenty years old, and Clay tapped the screen alive. A few more taps and there was a page with five faces on it.

"Whole world is looking for you. Also Clara and Wade Quinn."

"And Hotspur Chance," Faith said, finishing the picture.

"Prisoner One," Clay mused, barely above a whisper. "How the hell he ever got out I can't imagine. After everything Mallory told me about how they were holding him, it doesn't seem possible."

"How much *do* you know?" Faith asked, astonished at how in the loop Clay seemed to be.

Clay took off his hat and rubbed his matted gray hair with a dirty finger.

"We're what you might call the third-string bench-warmers. Not a pulse in the bunch, but we're on your side. Small group of twenty, sworn to help if help ever came calling. You know about Carl? We've been sending provisions up there for years."

Dylan looked at Faith: *I'll take this one.*

"Listen, Clay. Carl's dead. Clooger's dead, too, if you know who that is. The entire single-pulse army Meredith trained up—they're all gone. You're looking at the sum total of the revolution front line. We're all that's left."

Clay sighed and put an elbow on the table. His forehead fell into his open palm.

"I figured it was bad. Not this bad."

Faith explained everything about Jade and Hawk and Hotspur and the Quinns, the whole ball of wax, and then she asked Clay a question.

"Are you still with us?"

Clay didn't hesitate to reply.

"Absolutely, a hundred percent. Also, I'm sorry for shooting you both. But I knew it wasn't going to kill you. I was pretty sure, anyway."

Dylan and Faith both smirked and looked at each other. They'd just signed on with a guy who had a very itchy trigger finger. It wouldn't take much for Clay to start shooting if things went off the rails, not that it would do any good in a confrontation with the Quinns.

"I have something I need you to do for me," Faith said, sensing how long Clay and his team of urban cowboys had waited to actually be of some use. "You and your team."

Clay smiled under that fabulously wild mustache and his thick eyebrows rose in anticipation.

"Fire when ready."

Chapter 8

If 6 Was 9

They spent the next hour with Clay in the makeshift fort, sharing what they knew about past events. Too many of the stories ended with a dead person on their team and after a while they gave up trying to find a silver lining in the journey they'd each taken. They ate together, reviewed some of Clay's old maps, and all too soon began feeling restless.

"There's something I need you to do for us," Faith said as they stepped out of the fort. "It might really help us."

"That's what my team is here for, last resort," Clay said. "As long as it don't involve running away, we're ready. We're *always* ready."

Faith appreciated the resolve and the patience of a man who could spend years waiting in obscurity, only to be called up at the deadliest moment under the worst of circumstances.

"There's not much left of us, but what we've got is solid gold," Faith said, looking first at Dylan and then at Clay. Her meaning was clear: *We're enough to get this done.*

Once Faith had told Clay what she needed and they'd talked a little more, she and Dylan were on their way through the urban slums of Portland. They took no one else with them and asked Clay to steer clear.

"If we encounter the Quinns it might turn into all-out war faster than you or your team can scatter. Not worth the risk."

Faith had given Clay an important but ultimately very boring task. The good news was that it was something Clay and the rest of them could actually do, it would keep them occupied and out of harm's way for a couple of days, and in the end it might prove very helpful.

"The two-way is cool," Dylan said, thinking about the seventy-year-old communication gadget Clay had given them. It was tucked away in Dylan's pack, another in a long string of pre-Tablet wireless devices used by millions of people before the States were developed. This one was connected directly to a similar palm-sized device Clay kept strapped to his hip next to a revolver. As long as they stayed within twenty miles or so of each other, they could use the two-way to communicate.

"Keep it in your pocket in case I need to contact you," Clay said. "I'll nudge you first, make sure you're not in mixed company."

"Nudge?" Dylan had asked, playing with the dial and the buttons of the two-way as Clay pointed at a small button on the top of Dylan's two-way.

"Press that and hold for a few seconds. That will send me a nudge."

Dylan tried it and, sure enough, the two-way in Clay's hand vibrated three times, then went silent.

"You'll feel it, but no one will hear it. If the coast is clear then press the bar on the side and start talking. Same for me—nudge me first—in case we hit a shit storm or I've got Hotspur Chance in my scope."

Faith had watched this interaction in silence, noting how much of a dude Dylan was. In the absence of Hawk, he'd fallen in with Clay and his nerdy gadgets.

That had been an hour before, and in that amount of time Dylan had nudged Clay four times, laughing hysterically each time Clay's tinny voice came out of the tiny speaker. The circuits or the transmission bounce or both were making Clay's voice sound as though he'd sucked in a giant hit of helium.

Faith was glad for the distraction, but it didn't soothe

her the same way it did Dylan. She took out her Tablet for the third time in ten minutes and searched for a signal, found none.

"I'm beginning to wonder if they're within a thousand miles of here." Faith sighed, discouraged by the continuous dead zone. She had also begun thinking about the inevitable communication with Hawk.

"Should we tell him about Jade?" Faith asked as she picked up her pace and they continued between the empty buildings toward the Koin Building.

Dylan knew what she was talking about. "Let's see if he's left us a message first and if it's encouraging or not. I'm leaning toward not saying anything. It will only distract him."

"I agree, but are we thinking like soldiers or friends? I mean, wouldn't you want to know if the tables were turned and I was the one in trouble? Aren't we supposed to be honest with our friends about stuff like this, even if it's hard?"

Dylan didn't answer right away.

"He's in love with her, told me himself a few nights ago. That makes it harder to tell, ya know?"

Faith understood completely. If Jade had just been a friend it wouldn't have been a question. But Hawk was like Faith and Dylan's little brother, and he could get upset about things like this. She worried about him.

"I'm not sure we should have sent Clay on a

wild-goose chase." Dylan changed the subject.

"It will keep them occupied," Faith said. "And out of the fray. That's about all we can hope for at this point with a zero-pulse backup team."

Dylan nodded. "They wouldn't stand a chance against Clara or Wade, but if they cornered Hotspur Chance, different story. They could get it done."

"It's not worth the risk. Not after what happened to Carl and Clooger."

Dylan thought about it for another second or two and had to agree.

They walked a little farther, careful to stay out of the open as much as they could, and Dylan nudged the two-way. Clay's chipmunk voice carried quietly into the space around them, the speaker set at two out of ten. "What's up, amigo?"

Faith broke a smile at the sound of Clay's voice, high and goofy like a cartoon. "Just making sure you're still out there."

Dylan held the receiver closer to his face. "You sound like a hamster. A hamster with spurs. And a cowboy hat."

Five seconds expired with no response, and then Clay's chipmunk voice returned.

"Dylan doesn't deserve you, Faith. Break it off. Do it fast, don't make him suffer too much."

Maybe it was the intensity of the situation she found herself in, or Clay's mousy voice, or the fact that it was the first genuine smile (half smile though it was) that she'd managed since the Timberline Lodge massacre— whatever the reason, Faith would find later in life that this was one of those rare, unexpected moments that would remain in her memory forever.

It might have also been the fact that when she checked her Tablet once more a signal had finally appeared.

"Dylan," she said, holding out the Tablet in its stretched-to-large size.

"Well, we know she's not back that way," Dylan said, a quick glance down the empty street they'd just walked. "We must have just gotten within five miles of her."

"No, it's less than that. But it's higher elevation. Maybe it messed with the signal. Only about three miles, up that way." Faith pointed west, in the direction of the ocean. She zoomed in on the satellite view, a function that still worked even out here, away from the States, because the old satellites had never been destroyed. They floated in space, delivering long-stored images to anyone that could tap into them.

"You're not going to believe this," Faith said as she started walking again. "It's the Oregon Zoo."

"Jade is at a *zoo?*" Dylan asked as he caught up to

Faith and took the Tablet out of her hand. What he saw was that the zoo was surrounded by a mile or more of green. "No buildings out there, no skyscrapers."

Faith thought of something else. "Plenty of cages up there to put a prisoner in."

"Guys, you hear me?"

Clay was back, but this time he didn't sound so upbeat.

"Yeah, we hear you," Dylan said into the two-way. "What's up?"

"We got company," Clay said. "Better get out of sight."

"What kind of company?" Dylan asked as Faith motioned for him to cross the street and duck into an alley.

"Not the kind we want, that's for sure," Clay said, his voice cutting in and out. "Drones, too many to count. The State is on to you guys. You want me to ammo up?"

"Let's have them take cover and lie low," Faith said, pulling Dylan farther down the alley and into a recessed doorway. Dylan nodded and delivered the message.

"Don't engage, Clay. Stand down and take cover," Dylan said. "And don't do anything crazy."

"Same to you but more of it," Clay said.

Faith and Dylan looked overhead, but they were standing between two buildings. They could see only a patch of blue overhead.

"There," Faith said, pointing to the farthest right side of their view. A circular drone drifted past, just over the height of the buildings. It was followed by another, then five more, and then the sky virtually filled with drones, blotting out the sun.

"There must be thousands of them," Dylan said as he pulled Faith back into the alcove by her forearm.

"How low can they hover?" Faith asked, thinking of what a problem it would be if they could descend to street level.

"Too low," Dylan said as he peeked out of the alcove. Faith looked around Dylan's broad shoulder and saw the same thing he did: a dozen or more drones were slowly moving toward them, a few feet off the ground, scanning every square inch.

"Hawk and Clooger told me about these," Dylan whispered. "Each one has a pilot sitting in the Western State. These are demolition drones."

"What's a demolition drone?" Faith asked. Whatever it was, it sounded bad.

"This is how they level zeroed cities. These drones are bombs, Faith."

The drones were six feet across, sleek and narrow like a disk, controlled by a series of six propellers.

"So you're saying they're about to take Portland, Oregon, off the map?" Faith asked.

Dylan shook his head, ran a hand through his thick

black hair. "And the Koin Building right along with it."

Dylan took the two-way radio out of his pocket again and called Clay.

"You need to get your people out of the city," Dylan said. "As fast as you can. We think they're planning to level it."

"Roger that," Clay answered. His voice was small and static filled. "We have an escape plan; don't worry about us."

The first detonation took place a few seconds later, about ten blocks away. They felt the earth shake underfoot as a skyscraper plunged to the ground in a pile of rubble.

"What if they hit a building and we're under it?" Faith asked, thinking of the worst-possible scenario. She could see the tons of concrete and rebar crushing Dylan in her mind.

Dylan looked around the corner once more and saw that half a dozen drones were coming down the alley from each side. They stopped moving forward and began spinning in a wobbly circle like dinner plates balanced on a pole.

"I think we better go," Dylan said, cracking his neck to one side and then the other. "These things are about to blow."

There was no time to run and the place they were hiding in was about to be blown to smithereens. Faith grabbed Dylan by the shoulders and pulled him in for a last kiss before all hell broke loose. She felt their combined power course through her like rocket fuel and saw, in her mind's eye, the peak of the mountain.

"Time to blow our cover?" Faith asked as she pulled away.

Dylan nodded and despite the risk of what they were about to do, he smiled. "Yeah, let's do it."

"Let's see if we can get them to follow us," Faith said. "Keep them away from the Koin Building."

The words barely escaped her mouth when the first detonation hit. Within a few seconds, a dozen more explosions rocked the base of the building they'd been hiding near. As it started to crumble, Faith and Dylan pulsed, flying up as buildings collapsed all around them.

As soon as Faith cleared the tallest building and found herself in the open air of blue sky over Portland, she searched for the Koin Building. It was easy to spot from overhead because it was the only pink building in the city.

"There," Faith yelled. Dylan spotted the Koin Building and they both surveyed the situation. Drones hovered in the thousands, clustered together like flocks of crows. They descended around buildings in clouds, blowing them up with terrifying efficiency. Everything underneath Faith and Dylan was being leveled.

"We don't have much time," Dylan said. "There's too many of them. It's happening too fast."

Faith looked to the river and saw a rusted-out tanker moored to the dock. It was bigger than anything she'd tried to move before, but she'd felt her powers growing and thought she could do it. If Dylan could hold an entire prison in the air, she could move a ship out of the river and slice it through the sky. She closed her eyes and focused her mind, but the first thing she saw was home: Timberline Lodge, and the jagged peak that towered above. She opened her eyes and stared at the ship, focused on its rusted metal surface with a crushing gaze. Dylan had started picking up debris and hurling it with his mind, taking out one or two drones with each effort. When the drones exploded in midair it was like a fireworks display of color and light as one would blow up another and another, taking out twenty or more in one cloud of explosions.

The tanker rose out of the water like the remains of a dinosaur dripping with mud and water, a metal beast in the shape of a great knife that could cut through buildings. Faith aimed it along a line of hundreds of drones and moved the ship like an arrow. It cut through clusters of drones, shards of metal peeling away until the ship was torn asunder, raining down metal on the fallen city below.

There were still too many drones to count, and they

continued moving across the city in a wave of violence.

"There are too many!" Dylan yelled as he came alongside Faith. "We can't stop them all."

Faith thought of what this would mean as she looked down at a zeroed city on fire. They would forever lose contact with Hawk. They would never find Jade. And Hotspur Chance would very likely destroy half of the American population. She thought of the mountain peak once more—she just couldn't get it out of her mind— and then she took Dylan's hand.

"I have an idea," she said. "It's big. Trust me?"

Dylan squeezed her hand tighter. "What is it?"

Faith didn't answer. Instead she closed her eyes and thought of Timberline Lodge, the place she wished she could call home. In her mind her gaze lifted to the massive peak and she spoke.

"Move."

Far off in the distance, the mountain began to quake.

"What are you doing?" Dylan asked.

Faith squeezed Dylan's hand tighter still, every ounce of the power they shared focused on the mountain.

And then the unthinkable happened.

The top of the mountain, the peak she loved so much, broke free and lifted into the air. It was so far away they couldn't see it happening, not yet.

"Let's move around to the other side," Faith said, drifting toward the Koin Building. As the mountain moved, Faith and Dylan passed over the crushing power of drone explosions, until they were the only things left standing between the Koin Building and total annihilation.

"Faith," Dylan said. He could see the top of the mountain coming, and it took his breath away. "This is insane. You can't be doing this."

"We're doing it," Faith said. "It's both of us. We're doing it together."

Explosion after explosion rocked the city below as the onslaught moved within ten city blocks of the Koin Building. Faith and Dylan landed on the roof and watched as the mountain settled in overhead, casting a massive shadow over all that lay beneath it.

"This is incredible, Faith," Dylan said, awestruck by something this big in the air overhead.

The bottom of the peak released rocks and dirt like rain on a broken city as Faith slowly lowered it. Like a great cloud of darkness, it descended. Faith didn't drop it all at once; she moved it slowly, into the first explosion and beyond. As the base of the mountain came even with the roof of the tower where Faith and Dylan stood, thousands of explosions erupted. They sounded as if they were coming from underwater as the mountain shook. The sheer supremacy of this thing coming down from the sky blotted out everything it touched.

When it came to rest over the city, Faith looked up at the peak with its sharp lines of stone and ice.

"It's almost like being home again," she said.

Dylan just shook his head in disbelief. "Almost."

The two-way radio came to life with Clay's chipmunk voice.

"You guys really know how to blow your cover in style," he said, laughing. "We got out into the foothills in time. Thanks for the warning."

"Glad you're okay!" Dylan answered. "We're on top of the tower, heading in."

"Better hurry. No doubt this place will be crawling with Western State military in no time. Get out of what's left of the city fast."

They arrived at the base of the Koin Building and tried the first door they came to. It was locked, not surprisingly. A lot of urban buildings were locked up and deserted when the last group of people left. Portland had been, Faith remembered from history, one of the earliest pilot cities and had emptied out almost overnight. The Western State held lotteries with the biggest western cities. If a city could agree to come in all at once, its residents were given a better set of buildings to live in, more bonus coin for buying merchandise, guaranteed employment. All of Portland, at the time nearly half a million people, had fit into one-twentieth of the space it had occupied outside the State.

They circled the building searching for a way inside as Faith searched for any kind of heat signal that might represent a person moving around.

"Would the old alarm system still go off if we broke a window?" Faith asked anxiously. "Or is this one off the grid completely?"

Dylan didn't know. "I wish Hawk were here. He could tell us."

All the doors were locked at the street level. Peering inside, they saw that there was power from the old grid lighting exit signs and small corridor lights.

"Aren't we past the idea of keeping a low profile?" Faith asked. "Let's just throw something heavy through a window."

Dylan wasn't so sure. He looked toward the peak, squinting into the sun.

"I know we just dropped a mountain on Portland, so it's kind of obvious we're here, but I think that's all the more reason to lie low. If the Quinns are anywhere nearby, they might come looking for us."

"That would be bad," Faith agreed.

They milled around, searching for a broken window they could climb through and getting more frustrated by the second. These old buildings were airtight, frozen in time.

"Clay, how are you guys getting into buildings?"

Dylan asked, using the two-way.

A few seconds passed and then Clay answered, "Hang on."

They waited, Faith growing more impatient by the second, and then Clay was back.

"Doors will set off an alarm if you break the glass, but the windows should be fine. They're double pane, but you should be able to punch through one."

"Is it worth risking the pulse being detected?" Faith asked, opening and closing her fist at the excellent thought of putting it through a plate-glass window.

"It's so fast, just a blip. And you're down low surrounded by buildings—that'll cut the signal for sure. I think you go for it."

Faith didn't need to be told twice. She nodded and walked to the closest window she could find.

"I'm sensing you want the honors here," Dylan said. He didn't have to wait for an answer. Faith reeled back and punched the glass, hitting it as hard as she could with a balled-up fist.

Nothing happened.

"Step aside, little lady. I got this." Dylan's arms flexed as he pumped his fist, and then he let fly a punch that shattered the glass into a million little squares.

"I weakened it for you," Faith said. "It was ready to blow."

"Whatever helps you sleep at night," Dylan joked, flashing one of his million-dollar smiles in Faith's direction.

They climbed through the opening, kicking bits of broken glass onto a carpeted floor inside, and found themselves inside a uniformly boring office. Light streamed over rows of cubicles, each with an empty desk and a matching chair. Old computers and printers remained, boxes of office supplies that had never made it out the door, a golf putter that someone had left behind, a Starbucks cup.

"I'd have gone to the Western State if this was where I locked and loaded every day," Dylan said. "Talk about depressing. At least we don't have a nine-to-five desk job anytime in our future. Things could be worse."

"Maybe they abolished all cubicles in the States, but I doubt it," Faith halfheartedly agreed, thinking the exact same setup had probably been replicated a million times over inside the world of the States.

When they reached the lobby the elevator wasn't in service, so they started up the switchback service stairway on their way to the eleventh floor. When they rounded the corner for floor number six, they took a short break and Dylan saw a vending machine through the security glass in the landing door.

"Wait here," Dylan said.

"Dylan, don't—" But it was too late; Dylan was

already through the door and it was shutting behind him. Faith didn't see why she should wait, so she grabbed the edge of the door and swung it open about the time Dylan put his fist through the glass of the vending machine.

"That right hook of yours is going to get us into trouble if you're not careful," Faith said, but she was also interested in what the vending machine had to offer. Her stomach growled.

Dylan ripped open a box of Mike and Ikes and poured seven or eight of them into his mouth. They were hard as rocks, but they still tasted pretty good. He opened a Snickers bar and touched it with his fingers.

"It *looks* okay," Dylan said through a slurry mouthful of Mike and Ikes.

"I'm pretty sure the half-life of chocolate and peanuts is nowhere near forty years. Don't do it."

But Dylan took a bite anyway, made a weird face, and then kept chewing.

"I think I'll stick with the gum and the Life Savers," Faith said, pocketing a packet of each.

Dylan thought better of the candy and left it behind, but he did take a bag of pretzels before they went back to the stairs.

"These can't go bad, can they? I mean, they're basically twigs."

Faith didn't answer as she motioned for Dylan to

close his mouth and quiet down.

"If someone is on this floor they definitely know we're here, fists of fury," Faith said.

Dylan chewed as fast as he could and swallowed hard.

"Let's just go. No reason to wake an urban zombie if there's one living in this building. We don't need that kind of distraction right now."

Faith leaned in and kissed Dylan. His lips tasted like candy and she lingered.

"Okay, give me one of those Mike and Ikes. It's been too long, even if it is petrified."

They continued their journey up to the eleventh floor, pausing twice to kiss the candy flavor off each other's lips. Dylan knew the door when they saw it, because it had a Star Trek symbol knocker.

"Let me guess," Dylan said. "You don't know who Spock and Captain Kirk are?"

"Ummmm."

Dylan shook his head. "It's a good thing your kisses taste so sweet. You're not so hot in the retro nerd department."

"You're spending too much time with Hawk," Faith said. "It's turning you into a dork."

The geeky banter was helping Faith feel better and more herself, less focused on all the bad things that had happened. It made her feel guilty, as if she should be sitting in a room crying all day instead of eating candy and kissing Dylan.

"No way this door is going to be unlocked," Faith said. "Do we break it down?"

"I have a sugar high going," Dylan said. "Let me see if I can do it without using a pulse."

Dylan moved to the other side of the hall and bolted for the door, shoulder lowered. The door jamb cracked but didn't break, so he tried again. This time the door flew open and they entered the most unique apartment either of them had ever seen. It was sleek and open, with floor-to-ceiling windows that seemed to go on forever covering the back wall. The floor was white tile. A few pieces of modern furniture dotted the space, but the room was mostly filled with hip-high platforms holding different pieces of technology hardware. There were placards that described what sat on top of each platform.

"This guy really was loaded," Dylan said as he looked around. "It doesn't look like he even lived here. It's just a space to keep a collection of stuff and throw a party once in a while."

"This one has electric power," Faith said, picking up a gray cord and dangling it like a tail. "Talk about ancient. Can you imagine having to plug our Tablets in? That would be . . . *weird.*"

They searched the room and found more computers

with cords. Half a dozen Mac models, lots of old PCs, and a whole wall full of Tablets.

"Check it out," Dylan said, his eyes lighting up. "An iPad."

"First-generation Tablet," Faith said, also feeling a slight pang of nostalgia for something so old and foundational to her way of life.

"That Steve Jobs guy was a genius, no doubt," Dylan said, mesmerized by everything he saw.

"There," Faith said, reaching out and taking a Tablet with a dust-covered black casing. It was four by six inches, thin, not bad to look at. "This is it. The Tablet Hawk said we'd find."

Faith looked at the expansive window and knew that if the Tablet still worked, it would have been charged by the solar energy over these many years. She found a button on the top edge and pressed it, holding for a few seconds. The screen came to life.

"I hope it has a better shelf life than a Snickers bar," Dylan said. They moved to the leather couch together and let the sunlight warm their faces as the Tablet booted up. Faith ran her forearm across the glass screen, wiping away dust that had gathered for decades.

"I can't believe all this stuff got left behind. It's crazy," Faith said. "I guess even the super rich had to leave things behind when they transitioned into the States."

"As I recall, Paul Allen was worth like a trillion dol-
lars. This was probably one of twenty places he owned.
A guy like that? He was part of the problem. Who needs
twenty houses and warehouses full of possessions?
Rules are rules with the States—you get one bag, period.
This guy had more important things to carry."

"He probably filled his one bag with diamonds,"
Faith said, thinking as she often had about what she
would take inside if she had only one bag. "Books. I'd
take books. Those are the real treasures."

"Nice view," Dylan said. "Maybe we should move
here when we finish saving the world."

Faith had closed her eyes, letting the sun wash over
her, but her eyes flashed open at the idea of living in the
city. She hoped he wasn't serious.

"If it's okay with you, I'd like to go back to the lodge.
The mountains agree with me."

Dylan nodded. "We can come down here and get
candy on the weekends and play video games on these
old computers."

"And search for zombies and watch *Star Trek*
reruns," Faith added, starting to see a distant future in
which happiness in silly, useless things might be found
after all.

Dylan kissed her and touched her face as the Tablet
sent out a soft *ping* sound, like a tiny bell being struck
three times.

"Here we go," Faith said as she began searching for the network settings. She found them quickly and began entering the codes Hawk had provided them with.

Relay one: 342459
Relay two: PPd23ed
Relay three: WS404.12.7.8

A user-name and password screen appeared, and Dylan pulled out his own Tablet, reading off the information he'd stored there.

"User name is paulallen@itsme.com."

"Password is if6was9," Faith said, typing the password in as she said it.

They both watched as a small, spinning wheel appeared on the screen. It was searching for mail.

"Slow," Dylan said as he waited impatiently for the message they hoped had arrived.

"Three routes, all different systems," Faith said. "Still, shouldn't take more than ten seconds."

"I love it when you speak nerd to me," Dylan joked. "Don't stop."

The wheel stopped spinning before Faith could come up with another goofy thing to say and a message appeared. It was from airwalk@stalefish.ws.

"It worked," Dylan said, surprised once again at Hawk's ability to hack into things. "We just bypassed the most secure data system in the world and found our little buddy. Awesome."

"He once bought me jeans on the State system for almost nothing," Faith said. "The Western State can't hold Hawk, at least not digitally."

They leaned close, their heads touching softly as they peered into the screen and read Hawk's message from inside the Western State.

> *Why didn't someone tell me this place was so kickass? Check it out!*

Dylan clicked on an animated GIF Hawk had attached, expanding its size and showing the inside of a vast room filled with row after row of rack-mounted server hardware. Thick ropes of blue cord snaked along the floor as thousands of red and green server lights flashed.

"I was thinking he'd take pictures of State Disneyland or a five-D movie theater," Faith said. "Should have known better."

"He's found hacker nirvana. That's gotta be a good thing." Dylan tapped the animated image back to small and Faith read the next section of Hawk's message.

> *They took me straight into testing when I showed up, must be a thing they do. I completely wiped my Tablet*

before heading in, but man, they had a load of prebaked questions designed to trip me up. They're on high alert with everything going down. They even body-scanned me in case I swallowed a bomb. So that was weird.

They bought my story—I liked it outside the States until the crazy wolves showed up and I couldn't leave my house anymore—and I checked out clean of any nefarious activity. Then they took me to an intake room with metal walls and a white table and a guy in a white lab coat tapped a few commands onto his Tablet. My Tablet screen filled with a test that was obviously for monkeys and dipshits (tell Clooger he would have failed it).

Faith stopped reading and looked first out the wide window and then at Dylan. She had been thinking of how hard it would be to tell Hawk that Jade had been taken. Now Clooger, with his beard and big smile, loomed huge in her mind.

"This sucks," Dylan said. He put a hand on the small of Faith's back and shook his head woefully.

There was nothing to do but keep reading.

And guess what the first line on the test was? No seriously. You should guess. It said the following:

"Meredith told me you would be the one. I've been waiting for you, Hawk."

Noah's dad! I found the sleeper cell, or more like the sleeper dude! It makes sense when you think about it. Meredith would have sent someone with mad tech skills, and Neal Gordon has them. We messaged back and forth enough for me to know I needed to act like a normal intake. Then he started feeding me tests. He said he'd give me the answers if I needed them, because I had to clear for the highest level of coding work in the Western State.

But you know me—I didn't need Neal Gordon's help.

I answered the first round of questions and Neal Gordon faked an eyebrow raise and tapped on his Tablet a few times. Two more people came in and I thought I'd blown my cover. These ones were dressed in black, one woman and one man. They both said hello and nodded at Neal Gordon. Then he sent another test to my Tablet.

This one was also a piece of cake, more math and fewer visuals. When they all three nodded approvingly, I thought about backing off a little, but then it hit me. If I'm the smartest guy in the room, maybe they'll assign me to a job that gives me access to mainframes. Bingo. That's exactly where I wanted to be. I'm thinking to myself, even if it's low-level clearance, I'll be in the right place faster than I could have hoped for.

The rest is like the NASA space program: history.

I took four more tests, aced them all in what I can only assume was record time, and they assigned me as a trainee in the picture shown above—which just so happens to be one of twelve floors filled with communication servers. Here's me, at my new desk!

Hawk had taped a piece of black tape to one of his front teeth. He was sitting behind a desk not much bigger than the ones they'd provided at Old Park Hill High School with a giant grin on his face. Faith laughed, but a second later the laugh rolled gently into tears and she was crying, leaning hard into Dylan as he contained his own laughter.

"Why do we always have to be the bearers of bad news?" Faith said, feeling her wounded heart unravel all over again.

"We don't have to tell him, Faith. We could wait."

Faith wiped her tears and stared hard at Dylan, slowly shaking her head. "What if we don't make it? What if Clara and Wade and Hotspur Chance finish us off? I know it seems impossible, but it *is* possible. And if it happens then Hawk will be trapped in there and never know what happened to everyone. For the rest of his life he'll send out messages, and for the rest of his life he'll get silence and emptiness in return. We can't risk something that sad. We have to tell him while we still know we can."

Dylan nodded, agreeing that while it was hard and cruel in its own way, it was the right thing for them to do.

"Finish reading it," Faith said, sniffing as she stood and folded her arms, staring out at the city streets below.

Dylan tapped the goofy photo shut and read the rest.

I've got zero clearance, but there are only six people working on this floor and they're spread out all over endless rows of server halls. It's like a rat's maze in here! And Neal Gordon has done some nice work here, guys—he's got me set up with access to what we need. All I have to do now is hack, hack, hack. And more good news: Neal Gordon GPS-tagged all six people working on this floor with a microchip, and that data goes directly to my screen. I know where everyone is. They put me on a programming task that would take a regular programmer like three days to figure out, but I did it in under an hour, so that freed up some time.

I can track where everyone is moving and log out if any of them gets too close; otherwise I'm in serious hacker-mole mode. The system is insane, in some ways good and others not so good. It's layer upon layer of code, stacked up like a thousand pancakes, a maze of confusion even I have to step back from about every hour so my head won't blow up.

Connection is fine, you can send messages and

I'll get them. Looks like the relay time to me is about twenty minutes per satellite. I've got it set to hold the messages at each junction so they look like they've died, harder to trace. Same deal with my messages back to you, so figure an hour delay or about that on any communications.

I'm lifting pancakes, one at a time, working my way to the bottom of the code stack. Down there, in the soggy syrup of this unbelievably complicated system, is where I'll find Hotspur's original programming foundation.

Best news of all? These guys are all on programmer time. They practically sleep in here, so I can work through the night and crash under my desk if I need to. And Neal Gordon is the bomb! He brings me all the high-voltage caffeinated beverages I can handle and takes on some of the smaller hacking tasks. Life is good.

Wish me luck—miss you both—gotta bolt!
Hawk
P.S. This was sent at 10:41 a.m. WST. Tell Jade I LOVE Narnia, it's the best book I've ever read, and I miss her and I'm sorry. And tell her Aslan is watching over her, me, you guys—she'll know what I mean.

Dylan pulled his Tablet out and checked the time. "Ten forty-one a.m. Western State Time earlier today," Dylan said. "That's quite a while ago, like four hours. And no other messages yet."

Faith didn't respond as she kept looking out the window. She'd moved closer to it, laying her palm on the glass and feeling the warmth of the sun. "We're going to get her back if it's the last thing we do."

"Yeah, we are."

They spent the next fifteen minutes trying and failing to write a reply that included all the terrible things they needed to say. It was a lot harder than Faith thought it would be.

"This is impossible," Faith concluded, and it was.

They tried once more, failed again, and agreed to think about it as they made their way toward the zoo and figured out what they were going to do once they got there. In the end, they could muster only the basics, and try to word things so they weren't technically lying.

Great job, Hawk! We wish you had told us you were going on this mission alone, but we understand. Let's get this job done and then we'll figure out a way to get you home. If we can save the world, we can spring you from the Western State. We have a beeline on Hotspur and the twins: Washington Park Zoo in Portland, Oregon. We're headed there now, already within a few miles. Clooger and Jade are not with us.

Let us know if you figure something out; meanwhile, we'll get close and hold.

We miss you, too. Faith and Dylan

They looked at each other for mutual assurance and Faith pressed send.

"Let's get the hell out of here. The walk will do us good." Dylan was more assured than Faith, because now he had an even bigger reason to finish what they'd started. "It never had a name," Dylan said, holding the old black Tablet in his hand. "Let's call it the Vulcan."

"Help! I've fallen into a sci-fi black hole and I can't get up," Faith said.

It did them good to joke around a little bit, and a spring returned to their step. Faith could feel the determination rising in her blood. She grabbed Dylan's hand and pulled him toward the door.

"Let's go get Hawk's girl back and kill Hotspur Chance."

Chapter 9

When Elephants Fly

They were quickly down the stairs and out of the building, walking toward the Sunset Highway and wishing they could fly. It would take them at least an hour to reach the grounds of the zoo on foot, but they were way too close to take any chances. The closer they got, the more Faith could feel the dark presence of Prisoner One, Hotspur Chance. Faith thought of how easy it would be to take him out if she could get within sight of him. That's all it would take, and then she'd snap his neck. There would be nothing he could do, because he was a single pulse who couldn't protect himself.

As they walked, they began to cycle through their options and realized that they didn't have many. The only plan they could come up with was to lure Wade and Clara away from wherever Hotspur was hiding and then circle back and hope to beat them in a race for the stronghold.

"What would Clooger do?" Dylan asked when they'd cut the distance from downtown Portland to the zoo in half. They had veered into a parklike setting full of trees and underbrush. The elevation was rising fast, and checking the GPS system, Faith had realized the Washington Park Zoo was at a much higher elevation than the city below.

"Clooger would take it slow," Faith answered, half out of breath as the path grew steeper still. "He'd do a bunch of night surveillance and use all the Hawk techno firepower he could get."

"Still no word from our man on the inside," Dylan said. He'd been checking the Vulcan Tablet every five minutes, just in case.

"He would have gotten our message over an hour ago," Faith said, a worried edge in her voice. "Why isn't he at least sending a quick update? It's not like him."

Dylan shrugged as if it wasn't that big a thing, not yet. But then he checked the Vulcan Tablet again.

"You doing okay?" Faith asked.

"Sure, I'm good. A little nervous, but good."

"He's going to contact us," Faith said. "He just needs a little more time." She reached toward him, but Dylan moved off a few steps and checked the Tablet again. Sometimes he retreated emotionally, just as she did, when things got tough.

Dylan checked the Vulcan Tablet for messages over and over again as they passed through the rest of the parklike setting and found themselves looking across a field dotted with trees that ended in a fence line. They'd arrived at the zoo without a plan, worn out from the long walk.

"Let's sit and think for a minute," Faith said as she slumped down with her back against a tree and took a water bottle out of her pack. As she guzzled, Dylan checked again. This time, there was a message.

"Hey, we got something. He's back."

They huddled together under the cover of trees and read Hawk's new message as the sun was dipping toward the ocean, ten miles away. There was a time, before the globe decided to do some melting, when the ocean was fifty miles away.

Six nineteen p.m. WST. Another two hours and the sun would be setting.

Good news—your location scouting checks out with what I'm finding on my end. But hey, before I get into this, make sure and send me a note that Jade is okay. I feel like a total nimrod for not asking in my last message—I was in a high state of geek euphoria,

*but that's worn off completely and now I can't stop
thinking about how this was all a terrible idea.*

*I'm crashing! Need candy, more caffeine. Miss you
guys.*

Okay, so you'll let me know, then—cool.

"I don't know how we're going to tell him," Faith
said.

"We're not going to have to," Dylan encouraged.
"We're going to find Jade and get her back. I know we
are."

"I like your confidence," Faith said, but she was feeling the heaviness of a secret she hated having to keep.
"Let's keep reading."

The message from Hawk continued:

*I found two interesting things so far at the bottom
of the pancake pile of code layers.*

*1) While they were building the Western State
there was an offsite software development hub located
in—you guessed it—Portland, Oregon. Well, not exactly
Portland, but close. When they built the light-rail system
a million years ago, they had to run it under a small
mountain below the zoo. At the time when it was built,
the train arrived at a station 260 feet underground.
Second-deepest tunnel in North America, halfway to
hell. Getting down there is going to be tricky, because*

I'm guessing the elevators don't work anymore and those shafts are the only way down. Amazing as it may seem, the trains will still run under the zoo, back and forth between downtown Portland. I know, weird, right? They're wired into the Western State mainframes, and I can move those trains from here using a software override. Now here's the amazing part: no one ever knew where that secret programming location was. I know only because I've bypassed a bunch of protocols and I knew Hotspur was planning something from the earliest days of the States' development. Everyone who knew about that underground lab and its purpose is dead and gone. Hotspur made sure of that. I've got a termination list a mile long in here—all dead, I've checked the State system. We're talking several hundred people here, guys. Whatever he built down there was top secret and complex.

"Did you get to the end of number one?" Faith asked. She had leaned in so close to Dylan she could whisper the words and he could still hear her.

"Just now, you beat me there."

"This is even crazier than I thought it could be," Faith admitted. She was feeling the darkness of every-thing stacked against them.

"Let's finish reading; we're almost done," Dylan said.

2) The fact that this train still moves and Hotspur Chance coded that into the Western State security system seems odd to me. Like maybe he was thinking if all else failed, he could somehow operate something down there from inside the Western State. I don't know, still sorting it out. But I'd say the odds of him being down there, under the zoo, in some sort of offsite bunker, are pretty high. And from the looks of these foundation codes for the Western State, he can tap into basically anything from that location. The downside for him? It looks like I might be able to put up a firewall he'd have to break through. It's also possible I might be able to control some parts of the lab. Undetermined, since I can't even see the lab on my Tablet yet. Working on it.

So, what to do? If you guys are already there, I'd stay put until I can see about controlling some of the parts under the zoo. There's something else here, I can't quite figure it, but there's definitely some sort of back door built into the core software foundation. I think there's a code basement only Hotspur knows about, but it's hard to say. Hacking, hacking, hacking.

I do have some bad news, at least for me. Records show that no one who's ever come into the State system has ever left. People have tried—not too many, but a few—and it just flat out doesn't happen. Once you're in here, you stay in here. I guess we knew that, but

*honestly, you guys, I might have had a little too much
self-confidence on this one. I really thought I'd be able
to get out, like, easily.*

*I've probably landed myself in a prison even I can't
get out of.*

Hawk.

Dylan looked out toward the zoo and the sun setting over the very top of the hill. The tree cover was
overgrown and gnarly, like a jungle over the fence line.

"We know where Hotspur is. Two hundred and
sixty feet underground. He must like enclosed spaces."

"We could collapse the whole zoo on top of him, and
if the Quinns are down there, they'd be under a mountain of dirt and everything that lives inside. We've kind
of got them where we want them, if you think about it."
But Faith knew the Quinns had a living, breathing ace
up their sleeve.

"We both know we can't do it," Dylan said, sigh-
ing as he ran his hand through thick black hair. "We'd
never be able to live with ourselves if we left Jade down
there."

"I know," Faith said. "We'll have to find another
way."

They began walking around the perimeter of the
zoo, searching for the entrance, where they would also
find the light-rail elevator. Maybe if they were lucky,

Faith thought, they'd stumble onto some sign of Jade or the Quinns that would give them the upper hand.

The sound of screeching filled the air and both Faith and Dylan ducked down next to a tree.

"Was that what I think it was?" Faith asked skeptically.

"Sounded like a monkey or a screaming six-year-old."

They peered into the trees overhead and waited. A few seconds later, shadows moved above and something leaped between two trees.

"Yeah, we got monkeys," Faith said. "I'm guessing those aren't the only animals living up here. They must have just let them all go when Portland emptied out."

Faith thought of the more dangerous animals, the lions and the tigers and the bears, and hoped they'd long ago died off or moved into the mountains to breed in the wild.

"Come on, let's get a closer look at the elevator," Dylan said. "It's gotta be that building there."

Dylan pointed at a brick structure standing next to the entrance to the zoo. It was outside the fence line across from an open parking lot half filled with abandoned cars, two zoo buses, and the remains of what had been a small traveling fair of some kind. Three lifeless kiddie rides sat idle and rusting from decades of northwest rain: a mini Ferris wheel, a carousel, and a roller coaster with four cars painted and shaped like zoo animals.

"Sad kiddie rides," Faith said, feeling a pang of melancholy. The whole scene looked like the tattered remains of a broken childhood. She was also thinking about how close they were getting to the most danger-ous people in the world. Two of them were very nearly indestructible maniacs with the power to move just about anything with their minds. The third was plot-ting some kind of destruction that might, for all Faith knew, terminate millions of people.

"Let's do some housecleaning before we move in," Faith said. "Delete Hawk's messages and log out of the connection. Let me see the two-way."

Dylan nodded and dug into his backpack, tossing a few stale Mike and Ikes into his mouth. He handed Faith the two-way radio and went to work deleting files and logging out of the Vulcan Tablet.

"Clay, you there?" Faith asked.

"You're supposed to nudge first. I thought we talked about this," Dylan said, only half joking.

Clay returned a second later, his chirpy voice turned up louder than Faith was comfortable with.

"What's up?" Clay asked.

"How do I turn this thing down?" Faith asked ner-vously.

"Turn the twisty knob on the tip there," Dylan said,

but he was only halfway paying attention as he worked while the monkeys kept screeching overhead.

Faith turned the volume knob down and pressed the talk button again. "Listen, Clay, we're in what you might call enemy territory. Do you know where the zoo is?"

A pause, and then the chipmunk voice was back.

"Copy that. I know the place."

Faith waited a beat. *Am I sure about this?* She decided she was and gave Clay an order that she hoped might be of some use. When she was done, she added a final detail.

"Wait until after dark to move, then be ready. Got it?"

Another static pause.

"Roger that. Project under way, making good time."

Dylan had finished the work on the Tablet, effectively cutting ties with Hawk. He put the Vulcan away and slung the pack over his shoulders.

"Let's leave the two-way out here. He knows what he needs to know. There's nothing else left to say and it's too risky carrying it around this close to a fight."

"Agreed," Dylan said. "Now let's go check out that elevator shaft."

They skirted the side of the parking lot where the rides were sitting, moving between the trees that surrounded the zoo. The monkeys kept screeching, leaping from tree to tree as Faith and Dylan got closer.

"I don't think they like visitors," Faith said, but Dylan just shrugged it off as they arrived across from the brick structure that housed the elevator. Between them lay a slab of pavement thirty feet across, dappled with broken light from the setting sun.

"Wind is up," Dylan said, watching the shadows sway back and forth on the surface of the parking lot. "Come on, let's see what we're dealing with."

Faith wasn't so sure they should venture out into the open, but she was just as curious as Dylan was. All their intel said Hotspur Chance was hiding at the bottom of the elevator shaft. It was closer than Faith had ever been and it scared her a little bit.

"Maybe we should wait until it's darker so we'd have more cover."

Faith hated feeling hesitant, but heading out into the open and blowing their cover sounded like a bad idea.

"We can wait if you want, but I think we should go now. I'm getting a bad feeling about these monkeys. If they know we're here, maybe someone else does, too."

"And the longer we wait the more time they might have to prepare," Faith agreed.

Faith took a deep breath and exhaled slowly, centering her emotions and clearing her mind.

"You ready?" Dylan asked.

"Yeah, I'm ready. Let's do it."

Dylan went first, Faith followed, and they made it to

the elevator doors without so much as a sound from one of the monkeys. This felt wrong to Faith, as if they'd been scared off or led away. Dylan went into the alcove that held the elevator door, but Faith stayed out in the open long enough to take a better look around. From here Faith had a closer view of the zoo grounds, which were overrun with weeds and wild flora.

"Um, Dylan," she said. "We have company."

Dylan turned from the elevator, moved quickly back to where Faith stood, and put a hand on her shoulder, instinctively trying to move in front of whatever threat they were about to face.

"Better sharpen up the ninja moves," Faith warned. "She's fast."

An elephant had wandered in close to the steel bars surrounding the zoo, its head moving in a slow-motion, back-and-forth pattern.

"You've got to be kidding me. They left the *elephant*?"

"And the monkeys. Don't forget about the monkeys."

"What is wrong with these people?" Dylan asked, pulling Faith into the shadows of the alcove. The monkeys began howling again, filling the trees with chaotic noise that sent a chill down Faith's spine.

"Something isn't right."

Those were the last words Faith said before the elephant lifted off the ground, its horn blowing in fear. A split second later the elephant was standing on the pavement in front of the alcove, staring at Faith and Dylan.

"I guess we can go ahead and pulse," Dylan said, flexing his hands as the muscles in his forearms tightened. "They know we're here."

The elephant started to move toward the half-empty parking lot and when it was out of the way, Faith saw something she wasn't entirely sure she was ready for: Wade and Clara were walking slowly toward the elevator. Their confidence was one of the weapons they used against anyone who tried to stand in their way: the focus, the steely eyes, the assurance of their stride. These were two people you messed with at your own risk.

"Stay close," Faith said. "And I don't mean stand next to me. I mean *close*. I won't retreat into myself if you won't."

She looked at Dylan, her gaze melting into his, and felt that special something again, as if she could move the whole world off its axis with the power of her mind.

"I won't leave, I promise," Dylan said. He picked up the first thing he saw—a pickup truck that hadn't been started in years, and sent it rolling sideways across the pavement, sparks flying off metal. It crashed into Clara first, then Wade, knocking them over like bowling pins before it smashed a hole through the metal fence surrounding the zoo. It wouldn't be long before whatever animals remained inside were roaming the streets of downtown Portland.

Faith followed suit, flying overhead into the open space and picking up three more cars, sending them into a swirling, spinning tornado of metal and firing them all at once toward Clara and Wade. It felt good to unleash her power, to let her aggressions run free, and she was already picking up the mini Ferris wheel as Wade and Clara dodged the incoming cars. In nothing flat Faith had the Ferris wheel turned sideways in mid-air, spinning like a helicopter blade. Clara had flown up close to Faith, unholstering what looked like a Luger. Faith sent the spinning wheel flying toward Clara and heard bullets ping off the metal chairs.

"Incoming!" Dylan yelled as he watched a zoo bus hit Faith in the legs, sending her spinning out of control.

Faith tumbled head over heels into the zoo until she crashed through a fence and fell twenty feet into the lion's den. When she stood, the roller coaster and the carousel were both coming directly toward her, landing with crushing force as she shot into the air and searched the sky for Dylan.

"Keep this up and your little friend is finished," Clara yelled, holding out her Tablet for Faith to see. "Tap of the finger is all it takes and Jade's gone."

Faith was in a fighting lather, her brain working at record speed as the tendril thoughts of her mind wrapped around Clara's Tablet and pulled it from her hand. The Tablet sailed through the air like a Frisbee and vanished into the setting sun.

"Really?" Clara said, eyebrows darting up and her chin wagging to one side annoyingly. Clara's scars only added to her brutal beauty, blending right in with her short, cropped blond hair and piercing stare. The only thing about Clara's face that didn't have any fight in it was her pouty lips, which seemed too soft for the package they were attached to.

For a split second Faith felt as though she and Dylan might have taken the upper hand, but then the voice of Hotspur Chance echoed through the zoo audio system and she knew everything was about to change.

"Your needless skirmish has the capacity to draw attention from officials in the Western State. I'd like to avoid that. Jade is fine. She's bolted to the floor by a chain and I am holding a revolver, but she's unharmed. Things could change at any moment: *Jade is fine. Jade is dead.* Only one word, but I hope it sends the appropriate message."

Dylan drifted closer to Faith until they were back to back, keeping their eyes on Wade and Clara. Wade had taken an interest in the elephant, lifting it off the ground and setting it back inside the zoo.

"No more excitement. No more trouble," Hotspur said, and this time there was an edge to his voice Faith hadn't heard before. He was showing some emotion of his own, a pinch of anger that touched the sky.

Everyone glided to the parking lot and stood staring at one another. Wade was the first to walk forward, all swagger as usual, smiling as if he'd just bitten into a crispy piece of bacon.

"I'd gladly go toe-to-toe right now if the old man wasn't so hell-bent on doing things his way," Wade said. He was staring down at Dylan, their faces not two inches apart.

"I never listened to my old man," Dylan said. "I fight my own battles."

Wade looked as if he was ready to take the bait, jaw clenching against those high cheekbones, and Faith worried for Jade.

"You could just let us have Jade and we could leave. We'd do that," Faith said, turning to Clara. "We'd leave and never come back."

This was a lie, of course. Faith had no intention of allowing Hotspur Chance to go ahead with any kind of plan that involved mass murder on a global scale.

Clara moved a little closer, the four of them now all in a gang near the entrance to the elevator.

"I really wish you wouldn't have sent my Tablet halfway to the ocean," Clara said, inching closer to Faith. "Always with the annoying gestures, Faith. One day you're going to push me too far."

Faith did some stepping forward of her own, coming face-to-face with the person she hated most in the world.

"You kill Jade, I kill you. She better stay alive."

Clara flinched for a split second, overcome by the supremacy in Faith's voice, but then she turned to the elevator and rested a hand on a revolver Faith knew was loaded with titanium bullets.

"After you, Princess. Hotspur Chance wants to see you, so he's going to see you. After that all bets are off."

Faith had thought it was impossible to hate two people this much, but looking back and forth between Wade and Clara nearly took her breath away. The heat of her frustration very nearly made her forget all about Jade and pick these two up off the ground, slam their heads together, and bury them in the forest outside the zoo. She turned to Dylan for the briefest of seconds and saw that he was staring at her.

"Don't give them any power over you," he said, and she knew exactly what he meant. She had to keep her cool. She couldn't become like them, vengeful and mean.

Wade demanded both the backpacks and Dylan and Faith had no choice but to give them up. There went the Vulcan and the Tablets and the Mike and Ikes.

"You know putting us both down there is like trying to hold a couple of nukes, right?" Dylan asked as

Wade used his mind to force the elevator doors open. "If things get crazy, you're going to wish you weren't trapped underground with me. With *her*."

When Dylan said "with her" he was looking at Faith and his meaning was crystal clear: *I can't control Faith Daniels. No one can.*

"Down the shaft, pretty boy," Wade said. "You don't keep the old man waiting. It makes him unpredictable in the worst possible way."

A few seconds later, they were all four floating down into the side of a mountain, 260 feet into the earth in a shaft lit by the light of Wade's Tablet. The elevator was missing, but the slack cables remained, dancing slowly back and forth as they brushed past. Clara was above them, flying down last, but Wade was floating down at the same level as Faith and Dylan.

"He's a single pulse, you guys know that," Wade said. "So we can't let you in the same room with him. Too risky. He's got questions, you've got answers. Just remember: we've got the girl, and she's one thought away from a broken neck."

Wade let the cold efficiency of those words sink in as he stared at Faith and Dylan.

"When this is done, we're finishing our business. The four of us. No running, no backing down. Right, Clara?"

Clara drifted down into Faith's line of sight and

tapped her hand on the gun in its holster.

"I'm up for that."

So that was how it was going to be, Faith thought. Regardless of how things played out with Jade and Hotspur, these two idiots wanted a fight to the death in the service of their own egos. With the entire Western State at stake, hundreds of millions of people, all they could think about was being the two top dogs in whatever rubble remained.

They continued on, farther under the surface of the earth, landing on a platform where a sleek train sat under a row of yellow lights. Faith thought again about whether it would be worth it to end it all right here, right now. She could pick up the train with her mind, bash it over and over again into the ceiling overhead, send a million pounds of dirt down on top of them all. Jade, if she was down here, would perish. Hotspur Chance, Wade, Clara, Dylan. They'd all be gone. But the threat, whatever it might be, would also be gone. And Meredith had made the threat sound as if it was bound to take a lot more than a few lives.

"You mind telling us where we're going?" Dylan asked.

They boarded the train, and Clara talked.

"Long before we arrived on the scene, he built this place. It's kind of insane. You'll see."

Faith thought about saying Hotspur Chance had

also made sure everyone who knew about it was dead, but that might have revealed too much. How would Faith know a thing like that? Because Hawk was on the inside, gathering data.

The train pulled away, gliding on a track as if it was still in service and always had been. A moment later the train stopped abruptly, lurching everyone forward.

"What the hell?" Wade asked. He tapped something into his Tablet. "Train stopped. What's up?"

Faith looked at Dylan. *Hawk did that. He stopped the train. He's getting closer.*

A pause, and then a voice as the train started moving again.

"Talk like an adult and people will treat you like one," Hotspur said, his slithery voice echoing through the nearly empty train.

Wade obviously couldn't stand Hotspur Chance.

"Moving again. There soon. Hang tight."

Wade looked at the rest of the group as if he was really sticking it to the man.

"What are you, nine?" Clara asked. "It serves no purpose to piss him off like that."

"Oh, there's a purpose. It makes me feel better."

Clara rolled her bright blue eyes as the train came again to a stop and the doors opened. It appeared to have stopped in a location that was not a regular destination, but instead a ladder leading down to a service point.

Wade went first, then Dylan, Faith, and finally Clara.

"Looks like Wade's running the show," Faith shouted up to Clara, hoping to get further under Clara's skin and drive a wedge between her and Wade. Clara responded by putting her boot into Faith's head. Faith's neck snapped sideways then back again. The narrow way down was dark and full of shadows, so she couldn't see whether Clara was smiling.

"Cheap shot," Faith said.

"How about you shut your mouth and keep moving?" Clara said.

When they reached the bottom Wade flung open a white door and motioned everyone inside. A long corridor awaited them with openings along the sides. Faith saw cameras moving near the ceiling.

He's watching us, she thought.

Hotspur's voice emerged from unseen speakers. He seemed to be everywhere and nowhere all at once.

"Almost there, just a little farther and we're finally going to have a chance to meet. I've been looking forward to this, haven't you?"

The thing about having a pulse or a second pulse was that it didn't protect you from being moved or attacked. It was for this reason that Faith and Dylan both found themselves being hurled with all the power Clara and Wade had between their two minds. Faith went one way, Dylan the other, pushed through two opposite openings in the walls. As soon as she regained her balance, ready to retaliate, a door slammed down from the ceiling, locking Faith inside. A small opening, maybe four inches square, was the only view of the outside world.

Faith sensed something bigger was wrong almost immediately. She felt dizzy and weak and, most of all, as if a spear was being thrust through her forehead. She buckled over in pain.

"I hope you like the accommodations," Clara said. "It was nice of you to give us a few weeks before finding this place. Gave us time to do some modifications and upgrades. Titanium walls, very expensive. Somehow I doubt you appreciate it, though."

The feel of so much titanium, the one physical weakness Faith had, was overpowering. She felt feeble in the knees and the pain in her forehead felt like a vise clamping down tighter and tighter.

"Dylan, you okay?" Faith's eyes had become light sensitive and she felt as if she were staring into the sun. "Dylan? Answer me!"

"We've got things to do," Wade said from outside Faith's cell. "Afraid we have to be going now. But we'll see you both again. You can definitely count on that."

Clara didn't say anything; she just dragged the gun filled with titanium bullets along the wall as she walked away.

When their footsteps had dissolved into a distant echo, Faith slumped down onto the floor and closed her eyes.

We need a miracle.

Chapter 10

Electrogram Madman

The cold titanium wall felt like something prehistoric and evil against the small of Faith's back. Like an ancient voodoo, it sucked at her bones and her muscles, drawing energy away into a humming metal death machine. That's what the titanium felt like, most of all: a death machine. She could hear it vibrating into her mind, loosening the screws, working its way up and down her vertebrae. She felt the room moving, as if she were on a boat at sea, and decided she might do better floating in the open air of the cell. As soon as she was no longer touching the walls Faith felt less as if she was going to throw up, a little more herself, and yet she knew already: *If I stay in here too long, it will end me.*

QUAKE ◄ ◄ ◄

"Dylan, are you okay?"

There was no answer, so Faith floated closer to the small square in the door.

"Dylan?"

His face appeared in the small window opposite the hall, and a wave of emotion crashed into Faith.

"I'm here."

She wanted so badly to hold it together, to show how strong she could be in the most difficult of all situations. But something about the possibility of losing her soul mate, her one and only, her anchor—it cut through Faith like a band saw ripping into a two-by-four.

"I think we might have messed up here," Faith said, not so much dejected as perplexed by the swift turn of events. "I thought it would be different. I thought we'd overpower them if we had to or . . . I don't know what I thought. Clooger is probably turning over in his grave."

"It's not over until it's over," Dylan said, his voice showing more optimism than Faith thought the situation called for. "Although I am having a little bit of concern about the floor in here."

Faith squinted, peering across the darkened hall.

"Are you . . . not standing?"

Dylan looked down, then back at Faith, and they locked eyes.

"Can't stand. The cell is filling up with liquid

185 ◄ ◄ ◄

concrete. Looks like it's going pretty fast, too."

Faith thought of what Clara had said—*modifications and upgrades*—and realized it wasn't just her cell that had been altered from whatever it had once been. She thought of how it would feel to find herself up to her neck in liquid titanium, every part of her body encased in the one thing that could undo her. The idea terrified her. It made her wonder how Dylan was holding it together.

"Clara!" Faith yelled without thinking. "Answer me!"

God, how she hated that girl, and Wade, too, hated how they were so powerful and how they loved to hold it over everyone who stood in their way. If these two ever ruled the world, the world was going to be pinned under the heels of their cruel boots. For some reason she couldn't stop blaming it all on Clara, because she knew it was her twisted mind that would have come up with cages like these. She would have wanted Faith to watch helplessly as Dylan drowned in a lake of stone. She would want Faith to watch when the door of the cell was pried open and Dylan was encased in solid rock, his head the only thing sticking out at the top, eyes vacant and frozen.

"Take it easy, Faith," Dylan chided. "Save your energy. It's a big cell. We've got time to figure something out before I'm in any real danger. And try not to say anything if this turns into a Cold War interrogation scenario. Hold firm. We've got allies."

"Do you now?"

The voice came from the hallway just outside the angle where Faith could have seen who it was. But she knew. She'd heard that voice before, sandpapery and a little on the low side, like a smoker twenty years into a good long nicotine run. It was a slippery, conniving, soothing, terrible voice.

It was the voice of a devil.

"I would very much like to hear about *that*," Hotspur Chance went on. He appeared then, right there in the hallway, unarmed and alone.

Faith didn't hesitate, not this time. She still didn't know exactly what this monster was planning, but she knew how many lives were at risk. She had made the mistake of not striking when she could one too many times. She put the power of her mind into one thought: *Put this guy's head through a wall.*

Suddenly the vision of Hotspur Chance glitched, like the VHS tape of *The Shining* back home when the tracking went out of whack and lines danced across the old TV. Hotspur's lips curled into an unfriendly smile and he lowered his chin. His eyes narrowed and darkened and he stared at Faith.

"I'm not really here," Hotspur said. "I'm somewhere else. Close, but not right here. You didn't think I trusted either of you? Although I must say, Faith Daniels, you disappoint me. I know when someone is trying to kill me with a pulse. I *invented* the pulse—I should know. It doesn't surprise me that you would have taken my life so quickly, without provocation or explanation. That was a mistake, one I hoped you wouldn't make. But as you can see, I took precautions."

The back wall of Faith's cell moved closer by a foot, cutting the size of the cell from five feet across to four in the space of a breath. She felt her lungs catch and the weight of the room shift in her mind, as if she'd been plunged deep underwater, turning slowly sideways. She could hear Dylan saying something, but it was garbled and distant. And then she heard Hotspur's voice, big and close to her head: *Don't do that again.*

Her mind snapped back to reality and she gasped for breath. Something was grinding up her spine, like a cancer moving through marrow, and she realized she was no longer floating. She was lying down, her back against the titanium floor. She rose like a girl possessed and her back slowly arched away into the air. It was like trying to pull her palm away from a vacuum-cleaner hose. The floor didn't want to let her go.

"I'm going to explain some things to you now," Hotspur said, his gravelly voice slow and steady. "I appreciate an attentive audience, so do pay attention. Your lives depend on it."

A glimmer of hope, Faith thought as she turned and held herself aloft in a standing posture. *Maybe he aims not to kill us after all.* She didn't think of Jade at all in that moment. She couldn't even think of Dylan. Her own instinct to survive had taken over, if only for a moment, in the terrible pain the cell had inflicted on her. She wasn't sure if she could survive if the walls closed in much farther.

"Holographic technology was a passion of mine. You might say it was my recreation, like playing video games or listening to music. What you're seeing is a manifestation, a mirage built from the energy that already fills every breath you take. There are enough atoms and electrons and molecules floating in everyday places to make me appear before you. I've moved beyond something as rudimentary as holographics. What you're seeing is electrographic. The same technology they use in the States for those useless entertainment devices. I make something as grand as this and they use it to broadcast reality TV in living rooms. Typical."

"So if you're not here, where are you?" Dylan asked from his cell. "And what is this place?"

Hotspur's electrographic image turned in Dylan's ·direction.

"I'm near enough. As for the facility, it has quite a history. These containment units were used for testing. The zoo was helpful in this regard; I never wanted for monkeys or mice. You'd be surprised how many animals are available when you're donating millions to a zoo. Did you know there was, at one time, a mouse with a pulse? Yes, I had a mouse down here that could move cheese with its mind. Astounding. Of course, the mice were in here, with me. You two are in the monkey cages."

Hotspur shook his head and smiled at the floor. "A monkey that can move things with its mind turns out to be a very bad idea. No control, none whatsoever. I barely survived Lucy. She had to be put down, and while it might come as a surprise to you, that was hard for me. It's hard for me now. The idea of killing the both of you, such gifted specimens—well, it's not something I feel good about. The truly remarkable among us should be treated differently."

"So let us go," Dylan suggested, though his voice wasn't full of any real hope. "We'll walk away, never bother you again."

Hotspur's electrogram moved within inches of Dylan's door.

"Be careful making promises you can't keep, young man."

A second electrogram image appeared next to Hotspur, sitting in a chair. The angle to the floor allowed Faith to see only the top half of the image, but she could see who it was.

"Jade!" Faith said. "Where are you? Are you under the zoo?"

Faith was hoping to gain any intel she could before Hotspur could stop Jade from talking, but it didn't appear that Jade could hear what she was saying and the image disappeared a second later. It had been only a perfectly framed mirage surrounded by a slightly glowing halo of light.

"She's a feisty one," Hotspur said. "Can't keep her in the same room with me or she'll do something underhanded. Just like her mother—totally untrustworthy. But I did want you to know she's alive."

Faith's anger rose in her chest and it cleared her head. *There has to be something I can do. Anything.* She thought of the world outside and all that it contained. So many things she could move with her mind, if only she could see them. But she couldn't. Hotspur had made sure of that.

"This facility is known only to a very few," Hotspur continued, getting back on track with the information he wanted to share. "I had it built at the same time the States were being constructed. Back then, the people in charge listened to me. They did whatever I told them to do. They trusted me, gave me complete access. Of course, that was because no one but me understood the complexity of what we were doing, but it was nice to be trusted. I miss that."

The electrogram image of Hotspur Chance paused. It seemed to be looking back in time.

"Regimes change and time marches on. Politicians get their hands into the cookie jar and start digging around. My plan was set aside. They said it was too radical. They said no one could ever know it was considered to begin with. They locked me up, but you already know that. Luckily by then I'd already terminated every single person who knew about this place. You might say it's my Batcave, my secret lair."

"You're a murderer," Faith said, trying again to rattle Hotspur into making a mistake. "They locked you up because you're crazy."

Hotspur's electrogram flinched in anger. "That is a matter of opinion. A *wrong* opinion. I alone know the way. I alone saw the course of action required. And I'm the only one willing to do what has to be done."

What's he getting at? Faith wondered as she looked back at the titanium wall that had moved and shuttered at the thought of it moving closer still.

"Do you even know what I achieved?" Hotspur asked. "No, how could you? You couldn't know that I alone compiled every piece of data from every large city in the world. The crime rates, the disease, the way massive cities grew and fell apart. I mined a billion pieces of information and created a blueprint for the perfect city. Scale is a hard thing. Cities grow like organisms, pushing out in ways that make sense only in the short term, and then not at all. I created a model that can scale to five hundred million people without undue crime, disease, or pollution. I did that alone; no one helped me."

"What is it, Hotspur Chance?" Dylan asked. There was an unexpected sluggishness in his voice, and Faith wondered how full of wet cement Dylan's cell had gotten. "What were you planning that turned you into Prisoner One? Why are you the most wanted man alive?"

Dylan already knew the answer to this question; Meredith had told them. He wanted to hear Hotspur Chance say it.

"Ah, now we come to it, the meat of the matter," Hotspur said with a mix of humility and sadness. When he talked like this, like a wise old grandfather, Faith could see how a person might fall under his spell.

"The only way *then*—the only way *now*—to save this country is to finish what I started. Building the American States was only the start. What other countries do with their megacities is out of my hands, but if we want America at the top once more, to be the leader of the free world, we have to show the way. We have to lead."

"Lead where?" Faith asked. "And when did this become about America?"

This seemed to get Hotspur's attention in a new, important way.

"Every place on earth is overpopulated. It's the scourge of the age. Too many people, too few resources. Piling them up like rats in a cage might work for some, but it gets you only so far. One of the cages has to go."

"Meredith knew what you were planning to do," Faith revealed. The titanium was making her brain feel like oatmeal stew, but she had a storehouse of resolve made for moments like these. "She knew—that's why she left you. Because you're a madman. Because you wanted to kill people."

A prolonged silence followed, and Faith wondered if she'd said the wrong thing at the wrong time. "First you try to kill me, then you insult me," Hotspur said at last. "And you haven't heard both sides of the story, have you? You don't know the lengths I've gone to in order to *save* this planet, not destroy it."

Faith wanted to say, *You. Are. Insane.* But she held her tongue.

"I built the entire technological foundation of the States," Hotspur said. "Can you imagine—one person that brilliant?" Hotspur's electrogram face lit up with excitement. "And I chose where to put the States, the land to clear first, the precise starting point. From there, each state spanned outward, the land like glassy water being hit with a pebble. And they grew and grew; like a ripple widening in a perfect circle, they grew. One of them is sitting on top of a buried weapon. The weapon is positioned in a very particular way, to intersect with the power grid used throughout the foundation of the State in question. And you know what the power source is as well as I do. It's nuclear. It's fusion."

"A chain reaction," Dylan said, barely above a whisper.

"I have long called it the chain *reactor*," Hotspur corrected. "Everything will be over in a matter of minutes; they won't feel a thing. It's humane—I always liked that. And it will achieve what needed to be done: half."

"Half the population gone," Faith said, still shocked at the idea of it. "You corralled everyone for this? No one is that cruel. No one, not even you, would do that."

"You think I'm wrong, but I'm right," Hotspur argued. He was sounding a little bit upset that Faith didn't see the merits of the idea. "The only way to be sure we survive as a species, as a *country*, is to thin the herd. I'm doing what no one else has the courage to do. I'm doing it for all of us."

Faith knew now that she was dealing with an outright madman. The States might not have been perfect, but the crumbling infrastructure of North America had been rebuilt and centralized. The world was emptied out and was doing a lot better. The States were working. But he'd had a vision, and he was not a man like other men. He was special, he was the smartest person the world had ever known, and he'd set a plan in motion that his God complex wouldn't let him stop.

"Meredith was wrong to leave," Hotspur said, quieter now, as if he really regretted having lost her. "She thought she understood what I was doing, but she didn't. She saw only in part, not the whole. I was right."

Faith realized something else just then, something so simple and yet so dangerous. Hotspur Chance was never wrong; that was part of his diabolical brokenness, the lie he told himself. He was sure he had never been wrong about anything in his life, and he wasn't going to be wrong about this. He couldn't be or everything he'd ever done would come crashing down around him.

Faith heard footsteps in the long, dark corridor and a few seconds later Wade appeared. He spoke first to the electrogram.

"I found this in Dylan's pack. Thought you should know."

He was holding the Vulcan Tablet, the one they'd used to stay in contact with Hawk. Hotspur's electrogram image viewed it warily, turning his head side to side.

"Bring it to me," he said.

"Did you know he's planning to blow up one of the States?" Dylan said unexpectedly. Hotspur's electrogram turned sharply toward the cell and Dylan moaned, his face dropping from Faith's view.

"Dylan!" She was sure that wherever Hotspur was

QUAKE ◄ ◄ ◄

standing, he had just pumped more wet cement into the cell. She was horrified as she saw thick concrete lap against the small opening as it rose. It was a lot higher than she realized. Dylan was down to a couple of feet of space at the top of the cell.

Wade looked at Hotspur's electrogram as it evaporated into thin air, then back at Faith. Wade seemed almost contrite in that moment, as if for once in his life he felt truly sorry for the things he had done and the man he was becoming.

"He's right. He's always right."

"If you think annihilating hundreds of millions of people is right, you're just as crazy as he is. He's wrong this time. More wrong than anyone has ever been."

Wade seemed to think about what Faith was saying, to really let it sink in. But he had been brainwashed by Hotspur. "The Western State had its time and that time is coming to a close. People will thank us in the long run. We'll be heroes. We're saving the world, remember?"

He turned and walked away and Faith listened to the footfalls getting softer, the heavy door opening and shutting. She felt helpless, trapped. She wondered how it was that things could go so wrong so fast. She wished she could hold Dylan in her arms and make the world disappear.

And then she heard a voice, small and barely

audible, whispering into her mind.

Faith, are you there?

She knew that voice, knew it like a little brother. Faith hoped against all hope that she hadn't gone mad in a room designed to destroy her.

"I'm here," Faith whispered.

It was Hawk.

Chapter 11

Firewall

Okay, take a deep breath. You're in a room made of titanium and you haven't been thinking clearly for a while. It's possible you're hearing voices in your head. Also, Hotspur Chance has been known to bore into people's brains and drive them crazy, so that might be happening. Get ahold of yourself, Faith. This is only going to get worse, but don't worry. You are not going to go insane.

"Faith, listen to me," the voice came again. "It's Hawk. Drift up closer to the ceiling, to the right of the door. Speaker."

Faith looked up into the corner, where she saw a circle the size of a pencil eraser. Could it really be Hawk, whispering into the cell? Faith looked across at Dylan.

"Hey, good-looking guy in the cell across from mine. How are you doing?"

She figured a little romantic banter couldn't hurt.

"Not that great. How about you?" Dylan asked. His voice sounded as if he was in the middle of a bench press, trying to hold up too much weight.

"I'm fine, don't worry about me. How much space do you have?"

Faith couldn't see Dylan's face, but his hand came down next to the small opening and he made the thumbs-up sign. His wrist touched the wet concrete and he pulled it away. Dylan was lying flat, floating near the ceiling. "I have about a foot and a half, but I think the pump stopped. Faith, listen to me: if I fall into this stuff, I don't think I'm going to last very long. I wish I had better news. You know I love you—forever and always. I'm sorry I got you into all this. It was a mistake."

"Don't go all sappy on me," Faith said. She was on the verge of tears again, but she pushed them back, swallowing the knot in her throat. "A really smart guy said something to me once."

"Oh yeah, what's that?" Dylan asked. He wasn't struggling as much in the small space and seemed to have calmed down.

"It's not over until it's over," Faith said with all the courage she could muster. "And I love you, too. Forever and always. Stay put."

"That won't be a problem," Dylan said, and Faith appreciated the fact that he always held on to a small sliver of humor, even in the worst of situations. He'd man up a sly grin on his deathbed just to make everyone feel better.

Faith moved up to the right corner of the cell, feeling the force of titanium as she got closer. Her head radiated pain that ran down her back and into her legs.

"Is this really you?" she asked, barely the sound of a whisper passing over her lips. It was the softest voice she'd ever used.

"It's really me," Hawk whispered back. "As far as I can tell, as long as we keep it down, no one should be able to hear us. They're not tapped into this line but they are listening out in the corridor, so whatever you say to Dylan and he says to you, they hear that stuff. I tried the cameras and monitors in the cells, but they were dead."

"That's probably because Clara Quinn covered the walls with titanium and made some other not-so-welcome modifications. Dylan's cell is filled with wet concrete; he's barely got room to breathe."

"That's cruel, even for Clara."

"How are you doing this?" Faith asked. "Wait—don't answer that, not yet. In case Wade suddenly bursts in here and rips out this connection, you need to know—"

Faith had thought a lot about this moment, how she

wouldn't let another chance slip by without telling the truth. But now she stalled, taking a deep breath and gathering her nerve.

"—we love you, Hawk, you're part of our family. You need to hear this from me or Dylan. Clooger's gone, and so is Carl. It was an ambush. They took Jade—that's what led us here. Your GPS tag got us this far. She's here and she's alive and we're not leaving without her. I'm sorry we didn't tell you before. Sorry we couldn't protect everyone the way we should have."

Hawk didn't reply and Faith thought maybe she hadn't whispered loudly enough or that Hotspur Chance had detected the connection and cut Hawk off. It was the hardest thing she'd ever had to say, and the last thing she wanted to do was say it again.

"Hawk?"

"Yeah. I'm here. Just give me a second."

More silence as Faith's head pounded. She felt herself slipping down a few inches, struggling to stay in one spot as the titanium continued poisoning her system.

"Damn, that's a lot of bad news," Hawk finally said. He sounded lonely, tired. "Clooger is really gone? You're sure?"

Faith took another deep breath. "I buried him, Hawk. He's gone."

"Where's Jade?" Hawk asked. His small voice infused the whole situation with a quiet loneliness.

QUAKE ◄ ◄ ◄

"She's here somewhere, not sure where. One of the cells, maybe? But I haven't heard her voice."

Hawk didn't answer for a few seconds and Faith could almost see his face, the way his eyes moved when he was calculating a problem.

"Thanks for going after Jade. I wouldn't have expected any less from you two."

"She's family. We're not leaving her behind, Hawk. I promise."

Faith felt a growing ache in her shoulders and neck. She rocked her head from side to side, trying to ease the pain.

"Can you focus?" Faith asked. "Because if you can't I need to know."

Another pause, but this time shorter.

"I learned how to shut down emotionally from the best. I can do this."

It stung a little bit, knowing one of her closest friends could see how cold Faith could be. But given their situation, it was the best she could hope for. Hawk was going to set aside his loneliness and grief and give her everything he had.

"Okay, listen. I'm going to go through this really fast." Hawk's on-the-job voice was back, albeit in a whisper. "I got down into the foundational code, stuff that hasn't been looked at for decades. It's an incredible tangle of spaghetti in there, millions of lines left for dead. Think

203 ◄ ◄ ◄

of them like ancient hieroglyphics. The coding is stuff they haven't actively used for a long time, but it was left there. Hotspur Chance never expected to have an Intel like me digging around in the formative DNA of the States."

"I like the confidence, but can you do anything with the information?" Faith said.

"I found a connection to the location you're in right now. At some point he must have been in the Western State, coding from this side of the line, if you get my meaning. I can see the whole underground compound on my screen, and I can do a few things from my end, like talk to you. There must have been people working in both places at one time. I knew someone was in the cell you're in because it's activated on the schematic. The room across from yours is also activated. The other cells are showing inactive, so they must be empty."

"So if Hotspur was in the Western State while experiments were going on down here, he could stay in contact."

"Yeah," Hawk said. "And, Faith, you're at ground zero for all things pulse and Intel. He might have started with rats and monkeys, but eventually those cells were used for human testing. Hotspur Chance discovered the pulse in that underground lair. He tapped into other people's brains right there, under the zoo.

You're at the source, where it all began."

Faith let the information sink in. Hotspur had tampered with human DNA. He'd gone deeper and further than anyone else had ever dared to go, unlocking powers in the human mind no one had ever imagined. He'd figured out a way to unlock hidden abilities trapped inside certain people, animals, and at least one mouse.

"And, Faith?"

"Yeah?"

"He did a lot of testing. I don't want to gross you out or anything, but there's a huge room down there just like the one you're in. It's like a football field."

"And? What's in there?"

Pause.

"The bodies."

How many people had Hotspur experimented on? How many did it take to lead him to Faith Daniels? She didn't want to know.

"What else can you see? What other rooms are there?" Faith asked, trying to shake the image of thousands of bodies lying in an underground room.

"Not that big. Corridor goes past four other cells, then the hall T's. Right is a control room, pretty big. Left are some sleeping quarters, a kitchen, stuff like that. Beyond the control room there's another room, looks like it might be another holding cell or a private study.

Other than the aforementioned football field, that's it. Everything beyond the area you're in is activated on the schematic, so I can't say for sure where they might be holding Jade."

Faith was trying to picture the whole thing in her mind when Hawk said something much more important.

"If you give me a little more time, I think I can open the cell doors."

For the first time in hours Faith felt a glimmer of hope and possibility.

"Hawk, that's incredible! How fast? When?"

"Keep your voice down, Faith. You'll blow the whole cover. I've got access to the screen to unlock, but I have to hack into the code in order to find the combinations. They'll be listed together, I can see that much. The bad news is it's very likely that if I trigger the opening, it will send out an alert."

"Wade and Clara and Hotspur will know," Faith surmised without being told.

"You guessed it. Listen, there's something else. Hotspur is planning something big. There aren't any details about what it does, but there's definitely a starting point and a complicated series of triggers after that. Whatever Hotspur set up, it affects the entire grid, all the way out to the edges of the Western State."

"The starting point is an electromagnetic something

or other, the rest is . . . I don't know, more electricity, I guess. He's planning to electrocute the Western State, Hawk. The whole thing."

Pause.

"I think you might be right," Hawk said, a sudden awareness in his voice, as if he could see now how that made sense.

"I know I'm right. Hotspur Chance told me himself."

Faith drifted over to the opening in her door and looked out. "Dylan, you hanging in there?"

She thought she heard Hawk say something about a firewall, but she'd moved far enough away that she couldn't say for sure.

"Hanging is the right term, I'd say," Dylan said. "I'm okay, just feel useless. You?"

Faith was dying to tell Dylan what was going on, but she was afraid someone would hear. She could only say "I'm surviving" and hope Hawk got the codes for the cells fast. She heard a metal door swing violently open and footsteps coming down the hall. Before Faith could tell Hawk to go dark, Clara and Wade were standing in front of Dylan's cell.

"What is this thing?" Wade asked, holding the Vulcan Tablet Faith and Dylan had used to contact Hawk. Dylan didn't answer and Clara banged the butt of her gun against the cell door. "Wake up, Dylan. Hello?"

"Can't get low enough in this cell to see whatever it

is you're trying to show me with this vat of liquid death under my face."

Wade looked at the angle of the space remaining inside Dylan's cell and had to agree. "It's some kind of old-school Tablet, solar. It's booted up. What were you using it for?"

Faith listened for Dylan's answer, hoping he wouldn't say something that might make them raise the level of wet concrete higher than they already had.

"Let me out of here and I'd be happy to take a look at it for you."

Clara got into one of her huffy moods and took the Vulcan Tablet from her brother.

"Give me that thing," she said, taking it directly over to Faith's side of the hall. She pointed the barrel of the gun into the small opening of Faith's cell. "Tell me what it is."

Faith wondered what a bullet would do if it was shot into the cell, and then her ears rang out as Clara fired the weapon. The gun blast was earsplitting as the bullet entered the space. It ricocheted off the back wall, then pinged back and forth against titanium walls and hit Faith in the arm, spinning her sideways. Her head hit the wall and she felt her strength plummet as she fell to the floor. She looked at her arm where it had been struck, half delirious, and saw that she was fine. The bullet hadn't pierced her skin. Then she heard Clara out in the corridor, metal-on-metal sounds of a gun being loaded.

"That was a warning shot. The next one is going to hurt, Faith. I mean *really* hurt. Now tell us what this thing is and why you're carrying it around."

Dylan's voice kicked in from across the hall.

"Hawk's in the Western State. We were using it to contact him but it stopped working. It uses radio waves or something like that, you'd have to ask him."

"What's the little brainiac doing in the Western State?" Wade asked.

Faith rose into the air on what little strength she had, back to the small window, and watched as Clara and Wade looked at each other with some concern.

"He's an Intel," Clara said. "He might be able to cause problems."

Hotspur's voice entered the corridor, calling both Wade and Clara back to wherever he was stationed.

"Don't go anywhere," Wade said, anger rising in his voice. "I'm coming back and you're going to tell me what you're up to."

"Or you could let me out and we could go a couple of rounds of mixed martial arts," Dylan said.

Wade backed up toward the exit and smiled. "Wouldn't take me two rounds to finish you off. One would be plenty."

When they were gone Faith went straight back to the speaker.

"Hawk, you there?" she whispered.

"Yeah, here. They're heading back because I just put up a firewall for incoming requests from your location. It's not going to last long—Hotspur's too smart for that— so I need to get busy on a second and third security level. He needs a connection to the Western State system to pull this off. I can keep him out, but not for long."

"Hawk, listen to me," Faith said. "When Wade and Clara come back, and that won't be long, they're going to kill one of us. I can feel it. You need to get these cages open. Fast."

"I work better under pressure," Hawk said. "Hold tight."

Faith lowered to the floor, stood in the middle of the cell, and just tried to breathe as steadily as she could. Whatever was going to happen, it would be very soon. She was too weak to stand, but lying down would only be worse. *Come on, Hawk. You can do this. Get these doors open.*

As if things couldn't get any worse, the wall behind Faith moved closer, cutting the size of the room in half. It felt as if the air was being compressed around her, crushing the bones inside her body. The wall didn't stop until she was down to a few feet of space left to move around in.

She heard Dylan curse from his cell and knew he was struggling the same way she was. Was it really going to end like this? The two of them being slowly killed while the Western State went dark forever?

"Faith Daniels, you continue to disappoint me."

Hotspur Chance's voice was back and Faith's head snapped up in anticipation of what he might say. She was suddenly alert.

"You know, he's going to perish like everyone else. Hawk is no match for me. He may be an Intel, but I'm *the* Intel. He can't build walls fast enough for me to tear them down."

"I'm not so sure about that," Faith said, trying to sound confident in the face of total, abject ruin. The doors opened at the end of the hall again, and this time something about their entrance was very different. There was some screaming and shouting. There were three, not two, people coming down the hall, and one of them wasn't happy.

"You're hurting me! Not so tight!"

Faith knew that voice: Jade was coming toward her as Clara's voice boomed down the corridor. "Kid, if you don't shut your mouth right now, I'm throwing you down this hallway and you'll never get up."

"You can't *make* me do whatever you want," Jade shot back. "Where are you taking me?"

"Jade, it's okay—it's me, Faith!" Faith yelled. Her head felt as if it was full of fog, thoughts and sounds swirling around, lost in between one another.

"Faith?! Faith!"

Faith heard but did not see as Jade pulled free from Clara's iron grip and ran toward the voice. Jade was short and small, and Faith could see only her head as she peered out of the square hole in the door.

"Where are you?" Jade asked, looking back and forth.

"Here," Faith said, in what she felt was a soft voice but wasn't sure came out that way. "I'm right here. Are you okay?"

Jade looked at the hole in the door and caught Faith's eye. Anger sparked on her brow as Wade and Clara came up next to her.

"Where's Dylan?" Jade asked, and now she wasn't looking at Faith, but up at her captors with a look that said, *You better answer this question the way I like.*

But of course they didn't. Of course Wade had to rub it in and Clara had to smirk.

"Dylan is right behind you, about a foot away from drowning in a lake of wet cement. Clever, right?"

"Jade, don't," Faith said in the most adult way she could muster: firm and direct but not condescending. If Jade went ballistic on either of them, used her first pulse to send one of them careening down the hall, say, the Quinns might retaliate. Faith had been smelling the bloodlust on them all day. Clara and Wade were dying to inflict some pain on the world. It was what they did best, and they hadn't done much of it lately.

"Little girl," Clara said, squatting down toward the floor so she was eye to eye with Jade, "you're on thin ice. The only thing stopping me from hammering you into the floor is your usefulness. And that's not going to last much longer."

And that was when Jade lost it. Faith saw it coming before it happened. Those narrowed eyes, that furrowed brow, those clinched fists. Clara flew backward into the door to Faith's cell. Her back hit first, then her head, hard, like a bowling ball dropped onto pavement. Faith couldn't see Clara's head snap back, but she could imagine the look on her face. She knew that look. It was the look of an alpha female who knew she had the power to end you with the flick of her finger.

Jade's body moved up into the air and then back against the wall, and she began to hyperventilate. Clara moved in close, lifting Jade's body up to her eye level.

"I don't need to kill you. I can just hurt you."

Jade used her mind to try to push Clara away, but Clara was too strong for that.

"We're here to deliver a message. Shouldn't we get on with that before the old man gets all pissed off again?" Wade asked.

Clara glared at Jade, put a fist against her breastbone, and started pushing. Jade struggled to breathe, pinned like a bug on a wall, until Clara's fist was so deep into Jade's chest that poor Jade couldn't even take in the tiniest breath. A little more and the ribs would start snapping.

"Clara, come on," Faith said. "She's a kid. Even you're not that cruel."

Wade moved in front of the small opening to Faith's door and smiled knowingly. His words came in a whisper, only for Faith: "You know how she hates to be pushed around. She's like an animal. But I can stop her. I can stop anything."

Wade didn't even turn around. He just pushed his sister to the floor with his mind and held her there, angry and writhing, smiling at Faith as Jade slipped down the wall and gasped for breath.

"Wade, let me go!" Clara yelled. Faith could feel the rage pouring off her in waves.

"Both of you, stop it. Stop acting like children."

Hotspur Chance's electrogram appeared. Faith was struck by how real it looked, so bright and detailed.

"I didn't bring you into this world to act like such fools. You have a purpose, both of you. Get what I need accomplished. Now."

The electrogram vanished in sparks of light and Hotspur Chance was gone.

"That guy is so good at leaving a room," Dylan joked from his floating perch near the top of his cell. "What a pro."

"Dylan!" Jade said, moving back so she could look up into the opening of his cell.

"Hey, Jade," Dylan said, moving his head down into a precarious position just above the flowing concrete. Their eyes met. "Hawk and I talk all the time. He's my main man. And he talks about *you* all the time. He thinks you're amazing."

It was as if time stood still, if only for a second, and Faith could tell. She could just tell, even by looking at the back of this girl's head, that she had smiled. Two hundred and sixty feet underground in the pit of hell, Dylan had found a way to make Jade smile. Faith would never forget that, the ultimate importance of an act of grace like that. It meant everything.

"Everyone. Shut. The hell. UP." Clara was on her feet again and she was breathing fire. "Someone is blocking the work we need to do and we're guessing it's that urchin, Hawk. He's the only one remotely smart enough to find a way in there. There's something you need to know about this situation."

Clara held the Vulcan Tablet out and tapped the surface, bringing the screen to life.

"Jade is dead if you don't contact Hawk and tell him to stop putting up firewalls."

Jade didn't react to this news. She seemed to have gone emotionless and cold, not wanting to let Clara know she'd gotten the best of her. Or maybe she was just scared. Faith couldn't say for sure. But one thing Faith did know: Hawk had heard what Clara was offering. He knew a terrible truth that no fifteen-year-old head over heels in love should ever have to know: *I can save the world, or I can save the girl I love. I can't save both.*

"What do you want me to do here, Jade?" Faith asked. She didn't want Jade to have to grow up so fast, but she needed Hawk to hear the answer. This was one decision she wasn't going to make for either of them.

"If I get out of this cell alive," Dylan said, coughing before he finished his thought, "I'm going to be one mad son of a bitch. You better run."

Faith watched as Wade looked up at Dylan's cell and met an eye staring back at him. Dylan could bring an army to its knees with that stare, and if Faith didn't know better, she'd have said that Wade was very happy there was an iron door between him and Dylan Gilmore just then. Faith could see Dylan was thinking about using his mind to drive Wade's head into the cell door, but it was way too risky. If he lost his cool and took it out on Jade, there would *be* no more Jade. She'd get caught in the cross fire.

"Jade, it's your call," Faith said, pulling the scene squarely back on course. "We're locked up. We're probably not getting out alive. You tell me. Should I log into that device and send a message to Hawk telling him to lower the firewalls, or should I tell the Quinns to go to hell?"

Jade looked at the floor. She looked at her shoes, one of which was untied. She looked up at Faith, and then directly at Clara Quinn.

"Go to hell."

Faith had to admit, this was a girl with some serious spunk. If she hadn't known better, she'd have said they were long-lost sisters. She shrugged, which took almost every ounce of energy she had. "You heard the girl. Not my call."

Wade shook his head as if he couldn't believe what he was hearing. He grabbed Jade by the arm and looked down at her: "Your funeral."

When Wade started pulling Jade down the corridor, Clara looked back at the last second and caught Faith's weary eye.

"Your funeral, too."

And that was when the miracle happened, the moment Faith didn't see coming. It was the one thing that had the power to turn the tide.

The door to Faith's cell clicked open.

Chapter 12

Quake

"Kick some ass," Hawk said, and this time he didn't use his small voice. He said it like he meant it. "Hotspur is busting down firewalls faster than I can put them up. Get Jade out of there alive—I'm back to slinging code."

Faith used her mind to push the titanium door open on hinges that had been rotting 260 feet underground for decades. The door groaned open like a beast waking up from a long slumber, and Faith Daniels stepped into the yellow light of the corridor. She looked down the hallway and saw Clara and Wade turn in her direction. They both registered shock and confusion and didn't seem to know exactly what to do.

As Faith moved forward, away from the cell, it

felt like shedding heavy armor. Weight lifted off her mind. She shook her arms at her sides, power coursing through veins.

She looked at Dylan's door, squeezed her eyes half-way shut, and put her hand up. A moment later the door flew open and a lake of wet concrete poured out onto the floor like quicksand. Dylan was out in a flash, flying in front of Faith, instinctively protecting her from the titanium bullet–loaded gun Clara was already pointing down the corridor. Clara fired three fast rounds, the sound deafening inside the small space, and each one of them hit Dylan in the chest, falling to the floor like candy corn.

Clara looked at the gun and seemed to take note: *Three more bullets in the chamber, wait for better odds.*

Faith could tell Wade was squeezing Jade's arm almost hard enough to break it. He pushed her forward, holding tight.

"Get back in your cells or she's finished," Wade said. "I'm serious, Faith. Don't make me kill this use-less single pulse. It's not worth it."

Faith faltered for a brief second, glancing at the cell she'd come out of and the hell it would mean going back inside. She knew Wade Quinn well enough to know he wasn't bluffing. He was just that heartless when he needed to be. When she turned back down the hall, Jade had ripped her arm free from Wade's grip. Faith and Jade caught eyes for the flash of an instant, and then Jade did exactly what Faith wished she wouldn't do. She put her single pulse to use on the Quinns.

Clara and Wade both vaulted upward like rag dolls, slamming hard into the low ceiling, then back to the floor and up again. Over and over, Jade bashed them back and forth until the whole underground world of the lair quaked and roared. The earth moved overhead, lights fluttered on and off, and still Jade pummeled the Quinns with everything she had. "Run, Jade!" Dylan yelled. He moved like lightning toward the melee as the ceiling began to cave in and Jade's power faded. Clara and Wade were fighting back. The surprise attack had lasted only a moment and they were about to take control again. Ribbons of rebar and steel peeled out of the ceiling and rocks tumbled into the corridor from above. The earth was moving under the zoo.

"He's in! Hotspur Chance is in!"

Hawk's voice came from the tiny speaker in Faith's cell. He was screaming. There was so much happening all at once that Faith couldn't focus entirely on what he was saying, something about running code faster than Hawk had ever seen, something else about an electromagnetic source under the Western State taking on power. But really, Faith was so immersed in what was happening right in front of her, she couldn't focus on anything else. Her mind was still bouncing back, finding its footing. It could hold only so much.

Dylan pulled up short before he reached Jade, because Wade and Clara were blocking his way. Faith had some but not all of her strength back, and she knew Dylan had to be feeling the same way. They weren't strong enough to stop them both, not yet.

Hotspur's voice boomed through the corridor. "Kill the girl. She's outworn her usefulness. The sequence has begun."

"Clara, don't!" Faith yelled. "I'll get back in my cell. Just let her go!"

"Too late for that now," Clara said. Faith could see her face in a full bloom of black satisfaction even from faraway, down a crumbling hallway: *Oh, how I've wanted to hurt you, Faith Daniels. And killing this girl is going to hurt you more than anything else I can think of.*

Dylan tried to break through Wade and Clara, but he wasn't strong enough to do it, and in that moment Jade moved gut-wrenchingly fast to one side, hitting the wall with deadly force. Her head snapped sideways and connected with stone, and then Clara was throwing her in the other direction, slamming Jade again. Back and forth, five times in the space of a few seconds, and then Jade fell to the ground like a sack of rocks.

"Now you know how it feels," Clara said, and Faith couldn't be sure who she was talking to. Either way, there was no reason left to hold back. The only reason there had ever been was lying dead on the ground. Rage totally consumed Faith, but she had learned over time and through many regrets not to let her anger overshadow reason. She was seasoned now; she was a different person than she had been. The Quinns had taken her parents, her best friend, and her protectors. Now they'd taken an innocent girl.

"That's enough," Faith said, barely loud enough for Clara to hear. "You've taken enough."

Clara looked past Dylan and smiled down the crumbling corridor. "I'm just getting started."

Faith felt herself being moved back toward her cell and pushed hard against the power of Clara's mind. Wade dove into Dylan, knocking him down as the two of them tumbled on the floor. Neither one of them would let go of the other as they struggled, using their minds to slam each other from wall to wall, closer and closer to where Faith stood.

"I see what he's doing," Hawk said, and Faith heard his voice as if from a faraway hilltop, echoing into her ears. She held herself free of the cell, pushing back against Clara.

"I understand how this is going to happen," Hawk's voice continued. There was a pause then, a pregnant moment of wondering, and then a sad release of all that Faith had fought for when the voice returned. "I can slow him down, but I can't stop him. It's too late."

Faith couldn't see Jade's body any longer. Dust and debris were everywhere and the ceiling continued to quake as though it might cave in at any moment and put an end to them all. She watched as Dylan failed to overcome Wade's immense strength. Wade had pushed Dylan nearly all the way back to his cell, and now he hurled him into the wet concrete pooling on the floor in front of Faith. Dylan slid, screaming as the one thing that could get through his second pulse washed over him. It must have felt like molten lava, Faith thought. It must have burned.

She had a sudden burst of energy and thought about how she should use it before acting. Faith didn't just act, she thought about the options before her.

The gun. The gun had to go.

Faith hurled herself down the hall with everything she had, releasing herself from Clara's power. She rammed into Wade's head like a battering ram, knocking him off his feet, and there stood Clara, reaching instinctively for the gun. Faith thought of Clara's hand and forced it toward the wall as the gun came up. She pounded Clara's hand into the wall over and over and the gun went off once, then twice, sending titanium bullets ricocheting down the hall.

Clara righted herself, taking control as Faith began to feel her power waning.

"One shot left," Clara said, standing with all the

supremacy she commanded. She pinned Faith to the
wall with her mind, holding her there as the gun barrel
came up between her eyes. She was, possibly, the most
dangerous girl on earth, and she carried it well. Faith
looked into her face and thought even the scars she'd
inflicted on Clara had made her more beautiful, more
in command than ever before. A warrior, that's what
she was. Confident beyond all reason.

This is going to be your downfall, Faith said to herself. Her expression was confident, not fearful. She was
every bit the warrior Clara was. *This is going to be your
undoing. You think you're unkillable, but you're not.*

Faith looked back toward Wade and Dylan and saw
that Wade was holding Dylan down in the mire of liquid rock, waiting for the end. She thought but did not
say *I love you, Dylan Gilmore. I never left you, not for one
second*, and then she turned back to Clara.

"Now would be best," Faith said, surprising even
herself with the resolve and volume in her voice.

Clara looked at her inquisitively, a half smile on her
face.

"Yes, I agree," she said, putting pressure on the trigger of the gun. "Now *would* be best."

Faith gazed into Clara's eyes and almost felt sorry
for what her enemy had become. "I'm not talking to
you."

Clara's head tilted sideways in a way that Faith had

seen before. She was catching on to something that wasn't quite right. *If not me, then who are you talking to?*

But it was too late.

In that moment the gun suddenly turned on Clara, pointed into her own face, and fired. And while the titanium bullet didn't pass through her second pulse, it did knock her onto her back, the gun flying out of her hand. As soon as the gun was free it skittered down the corridor, toward a figure who was moving out of the rubble. The figure picked up the gun with her mind, opened the chamber, and saw that all the bullets were gone.

Faith felt the full force of her power return, but she didn't use it, not yet.

She let her pulse simmer and grow as Jade came into view.

"Are you okay?" Jade asked.

"Yeah, I'm okay. Are you?" Faith asked.

But Faith already knew the answer. Meredith hadn't been a second pulse, but she'd had a knack for giving birth to them. First Dylan, then Jade.

Jade was no single-pulse girl. She was a second pulse and always had been. It was a secret given to her by her mother, her secret of secrets, the one thing she could tell no one until the time was right.

Wade's jaw dropped open as he watched Jade coming closer, and Dylan had his moment. He kicked Wade hard to the right, rolling sideways and lifting himself into the air. Faith and Jade put all their combined energy into hurling Clara across the hall and into the titanium cell. The door slammed shut and locked in place.

"Hawk!" Faith yelled. Her voice had to make it through the small hole in the door and up to the speaker. "Override the locking mechanism and keep my cell closed. Now!"

"Done," Hawk said a split second later.

Wow, Faith thought. *He's really good.*

"Someone needs to shut this thing down and fast," Hawk said. "I'm laying virus cable as fast as I can, but the system Hotspur put in place is reactive. It's hell-bent on electrocuting the Western State and everyone in it. I can only hold this thing back so long!"

Faith looked at Dylan as he wiped away as much of the wet concrete as he could.

"I'm fine; it's him I'm worried about," Dylan said. He was looking at the same person everyone else was: Wade Quinn. Wade was glancing back and forth between all three people in the hall with a concerned look on his face. He got up off the floor and Jade lifted her arm. Wade's head bashed into the wall like a tetherball and he registered fury.

"Get in the cell, Wade," Dylan said. "Either that or we're going to make you get in the cell. Your call."

Wade wasn't the type to back down in a fight, even one he knew he couldn't win, so he went a little crazy.

He put everything he had into punching and kicking his way out of the corridor, but it didn't take long for three second pulses to throw him into the cell Dylan had been in and secure the door. Humiliated, Wade screamed and threw himself against the walls, but these were cells made for people who had the pulse. Wade Quinn wasn't going anywhere once Hawk was in control of the door.

"You're a little trickster," Dylan said to Jade, flashing a smile full of teeth even as Faith knew he must be hurting.

"Mom told me not to tell anyone. Not ever. She said I'd know when to use it."

Dylan pulled her into a hug and winced. "Good old Mom. She knew what she was doing, I guess."

"Your arms are burned," Jade said. "They got through."

Dylan wiped a hand across his forearm and saw the red stain of having been breached. The burns ran all up and down his arms. "Battle scars. It was about time I got a few."

Jade smiled up at him, and they both looked at Faith.

"I think you two should stay here and make sure our newly minted prisoners don't escape," Faith said, a new kind of command in her voice. It was the voice of a leader, not a person fueled only by anger. She looked down the hall. "I need to do this alone."

Jade wasn't about to question Faith on this one, and Dylan was weakened more than he was letting on. It was true, they needed to keep two of them outside the cells—it was too risky to do anything less. Hotspur was a single pulse. There would be no weapon he could throw at Faith that could kill her, and he would be unprotected.

"Are you sure you can handle this alone?" Dylan asked. His voice didn't have the usual strength and his movements were still choppy and slow. He needed time to recover.

"You get your strength back," Faith said, backing up toward the far end of the underground prison. "I'll deal with Hotspur Chance."

Chapter 13

I'm Your Hitler. I'm Your Stalin

Faith found three doors and checked them all as she moved down a narrow corridor lined with pipes and cords. The first two doors revealed rooms of machinery and boxes and looked to her like places that had once been occupied by computer programmers. The last door had been locked, but that was easily dealt with. Faith was at her full strength again. She backed up twenty feet, curled into a cannonball, and flew into it. The door exploded open as if the lock was made of toothpicks.

She knew something was wrong the moment she got her bearings and stood in the control room where Hotspur Chance was working. There was little doubt Hotspur knew what was going on. He was a master of surveillance and there were cameras everywhere.

It was immediately apparent that a genius was at work. Or was it twenty of them? This was the quandary that faced Faith as she looked around and saw not one but many Hotspur Chances working at various input stations around the circular room. All of them turned at once, an identical rueful smile on their many faces.

"You broke down my door," they all said. Twenty Hotspurs smiled. "And you've imprisoned my children." They waved their hands into the air. "Ahhh, it's all right. They have been a disappointment to me. Some discipline might do them good."

The twenty-odd Hotspur Chances turned away and went back to what they were doing. *Electrograms?* Faith thought.

"I've got just a little more work to do here, and then we can talk. You can even kill me once I'm through. If you can find me."

Faith walked to the first Hotspur she saw and ran a hand through its head. Her hand cut through the image as if it was moving through dusty sunlight. *One of them is real; the rest are not.* She slammed a hard fist down on the workstation and expected sparks to fly, but the station was also a holographic mirage, her hand slicing through air.

"Frustrating, isn't it?" Hotspur said. His voice reverberated strangely, twenty voices on top of one another in precise unison. Three Hotspurs and their workstations vanished, then reappeared in the center of the circular room. "I'd like to help you, but I can't. I'm busy cutting through the last of Hawk's viruses. He's quite brilliant. More than I bargained for, to be fair. But he is about to fall. They all fall in the end. They are all a mere shadow of the master."

Faith moved from Hotspur to Hotspur, slicing her fists through five of them. They vanished and reappeared in different places. It was disorienting and frustrating.

"Did it cross your mind," they all asked at once, twenty guns being lifted off twenty desks, "that possibly Clara wouldn't be the only one with a weapon that could put an end to you?"

Faith stopped in her tracks and realized her mistake. She turned for the door and thought of running, but what good would running do? If she didn't at least try to stop this catastrophe from taking place, she would live in endless regret of how close she'd been to stopping a madman and of giving up in the face of bad odds.

"Don't worry too much," Hotspur said, putting the gun down. "Not yet anyway. I rather like having you around, keeping me company. And really, there's nothing you can do to stop me now. We come to the very end, as it was always meant to be."

"You don't have to do this. You could change your

mind. It's been known to happen."

Hotspur's fingers flew across twenty keyboards and Faith watched as carefully as she could, looking for an anomaly that would give the real Hotspur Chance away.

"This is the antidote the world needs right now," all the Hotspurs said. "Some pills are hard to swallow, but that doesn't mean they won't fix what ails the patient. No one will ever understand, and that's okay. I don't expect understanding."

"What if you're wrong?" Faith pleaded. She swiped her hand through another fake Hotspur and found herself wholly unprepared when he used his single-pulse mind to throw her across the wide room and slam into a wall. She crumpled onto the floor, and when she stood up, slightly dazed, only one Hotspur stood before her. It was holding the titanium-bullet gun, pointing it at her head.

"I am not wrong."

She'd struck a nerve, but before she could think to send him flying to his death he beat her to the punch, sending her one more time across the room and slamming into the far wall. *He's powerful,* Faith thought. *More powerful than normal single pulses.*

When she stood and turned to the room all twenty Hotspurs were back, working at their stations. They looked up at her, mournful and angry. "Did you know it's hypothetically possible to have the opposite opinion of every single living person and still be right?"

"So you're God, then. Perfect."

"Not perfect," Hotspur said, tapping wildly at the keys. He looked up and appeared to be contemplating the God part. "You're a history buff—I know this about you. Were you aware that great individuals, people you probably admire very much, had rather a high view of themselves?"

"Like who?" Faith asked in an effort to keep him distracted.

"George Washington wanted very much to be called His Mightiness. Columbus practically demanded that he be addressed as the Admiral of the Ocean. Can you imagine? The king of all the navigable seas? And what about Catherine the *Great*? Did you know she refused to open any letter that was not addressed to Her Imperial Majesty? Victor Hugo, the esteemed writer, demanded that Paris be renamed in his honor. The list goes on and on—any person who stands far above the rest has good reason to ask for such titles. But I never asked for any of that."

"You don't make any sense," Faith said. She felt like arguing with him, but she knew that would be a mistake. *He's trying to distract you. Don't let him*, she thought.

"So close," Hotspur said. "Just a few more keystrokes and our little man will be vanquished. A shame he'll go with the rest, in the blink of an eye. At least he won't feel it. Well, not for very long anyway. It will be over almost before it began."

Faith was simultaneously running out of time and ideas. What could she do?

"Ahhh, here we are, then," Hotspur said. "Just need the right number of zeroes—one hundred and twenty-two—and a one, and then we're all done. Finally."

Hotspur turned to Faith, one hand typing, the other holding the gun trained in her direction. *Which one is he?* She couldn't know. She was in a room full of gun-wielding maniacs, and yet there was only *one* maniac.

"I'm not going to shoot you, Faith," Hotspur said. As he spoke, one of his electrograms faltered. A clue had emerged at last. A halo bloomed around its body and it sputtered out of existence. "We're both going to die down here. We all are. Because the world needs someone to blame or it will go mad and spiral into chaos. Don't you understand? I don't need a grand title or anyone to worship at my feet—I'm beyond all that. I know what humanity needs. People need more than this event, so long in the making. People need someone to blame."

Two more electrograms vanished and Hotspur's finger kept hitting the zero key. He knew how many he was typing in.

Seventeen Hotspur Chances looked into Faith's eyes with a destructive sadness, a willful defiance against humanity. "I am your Hitler. I am your Stalin. I am your demon, your death maker, your one to blame on down through the ages. I take this moniker willingly upon myself and I go happily into the great unknown because that, Faith Daniels, is what you need. It is not who I am, it is who you need me to be. Do you understand?"

He paused a moment and shook his many heads with a smile. "Of course you don't understand—no one does. No one will ever see the truth about all this: that I was right, that I saved the entire world, that I alone had the courage to do what had to be done. You are like children, all of you. So I give you what you need. I give you a villain to hate so you can sleep at night."

Five more Hotspurs plinked out of existence as his finger held in the air above the key, then moved across the keyboard to the number one, farthest away from the zero. His finger hung there and all but three Hotspurs vanished.

Three Faith could pick up and move. Three she could deal with, and so she did.

As his finger moved down and brushed the one key, she lifted all three off their feet and into the ceiling above. Two didn't move at all, but the real Hotspur did. His head hit the solid mass of wall overhead, crushing his skull, and he fell back to the floor at the only true workstation in the room. With all the electrograms gone, the entire room was virtually empty. Just the one station where a man could work and get things done, like murdering hundreds of millions of people in the blink of an eye.

Faith was about to move in for the kill, to make sure he was finished off, when his hand flashed upward and slammed down on the right side of the keyboard.

Hotspur Chance had hit the last key. The one key.

The screen he had been staring into flashed with light and code streamed in liquid lines. Something big and terrible was happening.

"You were almost fast enough," Hotspur said. "Not quite, though."

A bloody smile smeared across his mouth and Faith lifted him off the floor, dropped him hard in the chair at his desk, and moved his nearly dead hands over the keyboard.

"Reverse the code!"

But Hotspur's hands were as lifeless as two pieces of wood. He breathed faintly and looked up at Faith.

"What do they say about Faith?" he asked, and Faith thought it was a cruel final blow to play on her name's meaning. "I thought you could move mountains?"

Everything inside Faith burned with pain as she thought of the long journey that had led her to this moment. In all that time she had somehow managed to avoid killing someone with her bare hands. It was a line she had made sure she never crossed. She feared what it might do to her, how it might change her. But now, as she stared at the bleeding man in front of her who had terminated millions of lives, she reached out and put her hands around his neck. The skin was warm and she felt the big veins and the bones underneath. She felt him struggle to breathe and imagined his brain collapsing into itself, the cells in a deadly dance, searching for oxygen and blood. As she watched him struggle, tears welled up and ran down her face. She felt a storm of regret and anguish for what she was doing, for what this man had done, for failing to stop him.

And then it was over. Hotspur Chance was gone and she released him. She couldn't stop her hands from shaking.

And for the first time in ages Faith cut herself some slack: *I did everything I could*, she thought. At that moment she lost all hope in any kind of happy future, but there was a little grace, and that had been enough to keep her alive.

She looked once more at the workstation, from which so much destruction had been orchestrated. The whole screen had filled and more code ran in fluid lines across the top of the screen, pushing new lines down and off the bottom. Faith couldn't help wondering if each character she saw represented a human life being shocked out of existence.

Wait, that wasn't right.

Faith blinked hard, leaned in closer.

The lines of code weren't being added. It was an illusion at such high speed.

The lines of code were being *removed*.

Hawk's voice echoed softly into the nearly empty space. It was like a voice straight out of heaven, and everything terrible about Faith's life lifted in the space of a heartbeat. Six simple words, but for Faith they were the voice of a nerd angel.

"I think I have it contained."

Chapter 14

Shackles and Bone

"Hawk?"

Faith wanted to believe it was really him, but there was still a small part of her that couldn't trust it as she watched the numbers continue to reverse on the screen. She'd been burned by trusting people and things and feelings before.

"A little busy right at the moment," Hawk said.

"Did it start yet?" Faith yelled, but what she was really thinking was *Has anyone died yet? Has Hotspur's killing machine been engaged?*

There was a long enough pause to make Faith question everything all over again, but then Hawk's voice returned. "Not yet. It's like staying in front of a hundred electrified zombies coming at me from different directions. Good thing I played all those video games! I'm beating this undead code back into the ground. I got this!"

His voice was crisp and clear on speakers mounted somewhere Faith couldn't see. *This is really happening,* she thought. *We're saving the Western State.*

"I think I hear you saying you've got this under control," Faith said. This was one thing she wanted to be sure about. "So the zombies are the electrical charges Hotspur released into the State? And you're . . . what, like, zapping them?"

She couldn't speak geek to save her life.

"You got that right! The initial impact sent out charges that need to pass through a series of relay checkpoints. I've created a zero virus and now I'm tagging the relays before they can hit."

Silence from Faith sent Hawk into another code-slinging frenzy of hyper chat.

"It's a mistake, Faith. Hotspur Chance made a *mistake*. He was going for efficiency and speed, but he failed to put in any kind of backup plan if something went wrong."

Faith couldn't help looking at Hotspur Chance's face, caught in a twisted grin, and remembering what he'd said: *I'm never wrong. I'm always right.* The same thing had happened to Clara. They thought they were never wrong, so they didn't plan for it.

"Sounds like his real mistake was assuming you wouldn't be there to stop him," Faith said.

"Maybe so," Hawk said, but Faith could tell he thought it was something else. "I want you to understand this, it's important to me. All these electrical signals— zombie death machines, if you will—he pointed them all at one relay point. The smart thing about that? If the relay is open, they all sail through at once. It's an electric zombie apocalypse in the Western State. Not to be gross, but everyone fries at once. The whole system is infected in the same few seconds of time. But the really stupid part, the part I can't believe, is that he didn't plan for anyone to close that relay point. It never occurred to him it might happen, because he hard-coded this thing from the start. My level of hacking didn't even exist when he programmed this. I hadn't entered his imagination. Anyway, I closed the relay barely in time, and that's when it got interesting."

"Interesting how? You don't mean there's still a chance?"

"Nope, no, no chance. Even if I keeled over from a heart attack right now, this electricity infestation is toast. Go back to the zombie parallel—they all turn back when they reach the closed relay. They get confused. They start eating one another! Okay, that's seriously gross, but that's what happens. They chow right through one another until some of them leak out and then they hive, because that's what Hotspur programmed these zombies to do. They hive, and then they go searching for the next available relay. Mind you, all this is happening in seconds, not minutes or hours. It's fast."

"Can you keep up? Are you sure?"

"Don't have to. I just ran the last piece of programming and hit enter. My programming follows the action, watches where they're going, and stands at the ready with a zombie-killing wall of death!"

"Why not just shut all the relays down at once?" Faith asked. She thought it sounded dangerous to leave them open in case even one stream of electric energy found a way out.

"Can't do that. It would shut down the entire Western State. That's what electromagnetic shocks can do, and that would be a disaster of its own. Not as big, but definitely not good. Those relays are used for all the Western State's energy to move around the grid. Also, there are 3.8 million relay points. It's too many."

And then Hawk said something that made Faith pause and think all the way back to the roof of the abandoned Nordstrom with Dylan. All the way back to the beginning, when she could barely move a glass of water with her mind. Dylan had asked her a question then—*Do you trust me?*—and now Hawk was asking her to do the same.

"Trust me on this, Faith. I have it contained. We beat Hotspur Chance."

Faith nodded without speaking. *Okay, Hawk. I trust you. I really do.*

"Did I tell you I killed him? I killed Hotspur Chance. I did it with my bare hands."

A couple of seconds went by and then Hawk responded.

"Whoa."

"I didn't think it was right, using my pulse. It would have been like faking it, I guess. I had to really do it."

Faith looked at the body one more time and thought about what she'd done.

"Tell me she's okay," Hawk said, changing gears and facing a question he wasn't sure he wanted the answer to.

"Jade is fine, but you should prepare yourself. She's a second pulse."

Hawk laughed. A genuine, heartfelt, happy laugh. "I don't care if she's a three-D pulse. I'm so psyched about this! Tell her I love her. Tell her she's awesome!"

"You can tell her yourself."

"That's right, I can. She's alive. She's alive and Hotspur's dead. And the Quinns are locked up tight. Does it get any better?!"

"Speaking of the twins, I have a plan I'd like to run by you. Wanna hear it?"

"Do I ever."

By the time Faith got back to the cells, Hawk had already spoken to Jade and the Quinns had stopped trying to cause trouble. They'd thrown Dylan and Jade around some, but very quickly realized how useless it was. They were dealing with two second pulses. What was the point? Nothing they did was going to be enough to seriously hurt Dylan or Jade.

"I talked to Hawk," Jade said, beaming from ear to ear. "He told me he loved me. In front of all these people!"

"Somebody shut that kid up or I'm going to lose it!" Wade said. He put his fist into the wall a few times.

"Hawk stopped the program from running and you killed the monster," Jade said, totally ignoring Wade as if he didn't even exist. "It's been a good day."

Faith went to Dylan, hugged him, and felt her head slam hard into his.

"Clara, stop doing that," Faith said. "Save your energy. You're going to need it."

Faith wrapped her arms around his shoulders and felt Dylan pull her in close at the hips. She was trembling softly, an adrenaline rush still coursing through her veins as they kissed. When they parted she put her lips close to his ear and spoke softly. "I don't like killing people. I'm not doing that again. Ever."

Dylan nodded patiently and Faith went on.

"Are you ready to rumble?"

Dylan kissed her once more, close to her ear, and whispered, "I'm ready. Let's clean this place out and shut it down for good."

Faith could feel the power in Dylan's arms, the muscles rippling as he flexed. He was at 100 percent and so was she.

"Jade, I know you can't be hurt, but all the same, I'd like you to stand aside and let Dylan and me handle this next part. Okay?"

Jade didn't look at all happy, but she seemed to accept it, nodding defiantly.

Faith knelt and whispered into Jade's ear so no one else could hear, and Jade smiled again, content to have a part in what was about to happen. She ran down the corridor in the direction of the elevator that had brought them all 260 feet underground.

Faith stood and nodded at Dylan. He nodded back.

"Did you know everything Hotspur was planning to do?" Faith asked. Her question was aimed at Clara, but Wade was quicker to the answer.

"Terminate the Western State. He said it was what we were made for."

"And you were okay with that?" Faith asked,

staggered by the emotionless quality of Wade's voice.

"I never said I was okay with it. Who knows? Maybe if the timing had been different, it would have been me snapping his neck instead of you."

Faith's stomach dropped at the sound of what she'd done. She'd killed someone with her bare hands, and that would, in some ways, become a marker for the rest of her life. Maybe that's what she'd wanted it to be: the last dark moment of a broken past, the violent release into a better future.

"Clara had plans of her own," Wade added bitterly. "I never agreed to any of it."

"Way to throw me under the bus when we're both gonna die anyway," Clara said. "Very classy."

"Who said anything about dying?" Wade asked.

No one answered, which seemed to make Wade more nervous, as if the thought hadn't, for some reason, crossed his mind.

"You'd have come along willingly and you know it," Clara snarled at her brother. "And it could have been nice, the world at our feet. Doesn't matter now. Soon as this place falls, we're under a mountain of dirt and everything that comes with it, brother."

Dylan looked in on Wade, right up in the small square. "She's right, you know. It wouldn't take much to bring this ceiling down on top of you."

"So that's your plan, crushing us to death?" Wade

asked. He shook his head, feigning disbelief, and stared Dylan down. "I have a better idea. Let me out of this cage and we'll see if you can beat me in a real fight?"

Dylan looked at Faith and she could see he wanted this, wanted it more than anything. But there were real risks. They could pummel the walls enough to trap them all if the ceiling collapsed.

"We're not going to leave you down here to rot, but we're not fighting down here, either," Faith said. "Too risky."

She moved to the side of the cell door that was farthest from the elevator. She heard the gentle, deep thump of an explosive force far in the distance. Dust rained down from the ceiling and the ground shook slightly.

"Open them up," Faith said.

Hawk's voice pinged into Clara's cell: "On it."

The two cell doors clicked open and then there was a deep silence. Faith couldn't see Wade or Clara, but she imagined what they were doing. They were both looking at the open doors, thinking how stupid Faith and Dylan were for letting them out. They were, in many ways, just like their father. It wasn't that these two thought they were never wrong; it was a different reaction sprung from the same source. Wade and Clara thought they were indestructible, maybe even immortal. And it was for this reason that Faith imagined them with smiles on their faces. Things were going as they always eventually went. The only thing standing between them and winning had been time.

Both doors flew open at the same time with enough force to remove them from their hinges. The two slabs of metal careened back and forth against the walls with a chaotic violence that made Faith take two steps backward.

"Looks like we woke the monsters," Dylan said, flashing a look at Faith she'd seen before. It was a look that told her everything she loved about him in only a few seconds: *Let's kick some ass, I love you, you're beautiful.*

Clara and Wade stepped out into the corridor. They were closer to the surface than Dylan and Faith were now, and they knew it. Clara pushed her hands out in front of her chest, forcing her energy toward Faith. Wade gathered the quickly hardening coat of concrete from the floor and pulled it up into the air. It floated there, a melting wall of stone, and then Wade pushed it forward. Faith was deadlocked with Clara, the two of them pushing against each other, cancelling out their own energy. Half-hardened concrete exploded forward, crashing into Faith as Dylan unconsciously moved directly behind her. When Faith took the brunt of the blow, she stumbled back, but Dylan pushed forward and held her aloft.

"Never figured you for a guy who'd use a girl as a shield in a fight," Wade said. "Actually, that's not true. I did figure that. You seem like *just* the type."

While Wade was running his mouth, Dylan was tightening his grip around Faith's waist and turning her in the air, aiming them both like a rocket. Before Wade or Clara could react, Faith and Dylan launched, ramming into Clara's stomach like a double-headed battering ram. She buckled in half, carried away as Faith and Dylan pushed hard down the hall.

"Make her feel it," Dylan said into Faith's ear, letting her go. She felt his hands leave her side, pushing her forward, and then she dug deeper than she'd ever gone for power she didn't even know she had. It was like going from normal speed to light speed in a burst of energy, then stopping just as fast, letting the cargo free.

Clara flew forward, spinning out of control, and slammed so hard into a wall of mortar it collapsed into a hole. Behind the hole lay wet earth and roots and worms, and Clara didn't stop until she was ten feet beyond the wall. She'd punched a crater hole and the earth shook, raining down debris from the fragile ceiling.

When Faith turned to see where Dylan had gone, she saw that he and Wade were caught in a death spiral, clamped onto each other like sumo wrestlers, hurtling toward her. She dodged to the side and let them pass, a human tumbleweed making its way toward the elevator shaft.

Clara crawled out of the narrow tunnel and fell to the floor. She stood, wobbling back and forth, covered in dirt.

She definitely felt that, Faith thought, and it pleased her to think she could make Clara feel some pain. She watched as Clara took notice of her twin brother rolling past, bouncing into the open area before the elevator shaft. Dylan had let him go and the two stood face-to-face, ready to lock horns again.

Clara glanced at Faith, then back at the shaft, then back at Faith.

"You better run," Faith said, and she started to walk toward Clara with the resolve of a rhino about to charge. For the first time in their long battle over many months, Faith saw fear in Clara's eyes. She took flight, following Clara as she moved for the exit.

"Come on, Wade!" Clara yelled as she passed by and entered the elevator shaft. Wade was gone in a flash of dust and debris, up the shaft with his sister as Dylan and Faith took chase. It was 260 feet of tunnel leading to the surface, and at the top, the light of day shone through. It had a strange green hue, an avocado sky that didn't belong.

"Looks like Jade did her job well," Dylan said with a hundred feet to go. She had gotten outside and used whatever means necessary to blow the roof off the elevator shaft.

"Only question left is whether Clay was ready," Faith said.

"He's a cowboy. You can always count on a cowboy."

Faith flashed a smile at Dylan as they approached the top.

They could have taken a moment to embrace and release all the pain and pressure they'd endured. But that would all have to wait for another time, because right then Clara and Wade broke through into daylight.

Their freedom lasted only a split second as the air above the opening closed in on them. Clay's cage, which was a thing of real beauty and sophistication, was waiting beyond the blue. Clara and Wade ran right into it, and like any good trap, the door swung shut the moment they were inside.

Faith and Dylan slowed to a crawl and slid to the side of the cage, holding in the air and observing what a fine piece of work it was.

"You outdid yourself, Clay," Dylan said, circling the cage in midair.

Jade was standing next to Clay, beaming with pride.

"This little lady knows how to blow the top off a building," Clay said. "She done good."

Clay was standing on the pavement with his shotgun in hand, along with a small army of cowboys behind him. The cage itself was held aloft on four ropes attached to tall trees. Faith took a good look at the cage and found it was pretty much exactly what she had ordered, with the exception of the snakes. The cage looked to be constructed of a light steel frame, but it was everything attached to the frame that mattered: a thick web of ivy and green vine, teeming with snakes and squirrels and moles.

"Nice touch with the snakes," Faith said.

"Figured it couldn't hurt," Clay said, tipping his hat and smiling as he looked up at his own invention. "Rattlers. Mean as hell."

What Clay and his team had built was alive with vermin and olive-green branches. Clara and Wade were trapped inside a cage with walls that inflicted pain and sucked power. It was their version of the titanium cell Faith had been in, and it was having the same effect on the Quinns. The walls of the cage moved back and forth a few times, but after that, it was obvious its two prisoners had decided to give up.

"Did you do the other parts?" Faith asked Clay.

Clay only smiled and waved them down to the ground and across the parking lot. His whole team of urban cowboys gathered around an old-fashioned detonator: a red box with a T handle for pushing down. Wires ran the length of the parking lot and into the zoo beyond the gates.

"How much dynamite we got in there, Earl?" Clay asked, turning to a big-bellied man with a long mustache that looked like an upside-down horseshoe.

Earl chuckled, turned to his right, and spit. "Five hundred pounds, give or take."

Dylan whistled through his teeth.

"And you got all the animals out, you're sure?"

Clay nodded and held his gun up a few extra inches from his belt buckle. "A couple of members of the cat family, a few bears, mostly monkeys. And the elephant. They're all clear, roaming around in the back forty."

Faith had thought this through quite a bit over the past few days, and standing there on the cracked concrete she felt surer than ever about what had to be done.

Faith turned to Clay. "You're sure?"

"Only a few critters were left in there, most of them hightailed it years ago. We checked every inch," Clay said. "It's empty."

Two penguins waddled through the gate, looked back as if they were the last animals on earth, and headed for the woods.

"Okay, now it's empty," Clay said with more confidence than Faith was willing to buy into.

They all waited a few minutes while Jade did a quick fly over the zoo, just to make sure, while Faith looked across the expanse of the grounds and the park that surrounded it, four hundred acres of abandoned space.

"Dylan, I need you," she said, holding a hand out toward him. When their hands touched she thought of what they'd done in the fallen city, the mountain she had somehow moved with her mind. Dylan tightened his grip and closed his eyes, but Faith looked to the sky.

"What is that?" Clay asked. He heard it first—then they all did—the sound of something unimaginably huge moving off the ground in the distance.

"Come to me," Faith said. "Cover this darkness once and for all. Do it now."

The mountain rushed up into the sky and tumbled end over end in the air. It cut the space between the city and zoo in half faster than any of them could believe. Dylan opened his eyes and looked at Earl.

"You might want to back up a little."

"No doubt," Earl agreed, pushing his team back to the farthest edge of the parking lot and all the way into the woods.

Jade, Faith, and Dylan flew up into the air and backed away from the zoo, leaving only Wade and Clara in harm's way. The cage they were held aloft in was right on the edge of the entry gate.

"Don't do this, Faith," Clara pleaded as the mountain rapidly approached. "Please."

Wade used what little strength he had left to pick up a car with his mind and hurl it in the direction of the sky. It was a feeble effort, hitting the mountain like a spitball and crashing back to the earth.

Faith brought the mountain in low and let it hover and spin, dropping chunks of earth like rain. It covered every square inch of the zoo and cast a shadow over the ivy cage that took Clara's breath away. It was the thing that could end Wade and Clara, a monster of such breathtaking proportion it made them both cower inside the cage.

"Always remember, I could have put an end to you both," Faith said. "Right here, right now. And I chose not to."

Faith pushed her hands forward and the mountain pitched forward, away from the ivy cage and farther over the zoo.

And then she dropped it.

The sound was deep and primordial, a huge dust cloud gathering into the air as the concrete of the parking lot buckled. Faith felt a rumbling wave of power in the air—the *quake*—as a billion tons of earth ripped through the ground and the mountain settled into place. Everything under the zoo was crushed, demolished, hidden like a dinosaur fossil for all time.

"Hot damn!" Clay yelled from the woods off in the distance.

When all the dust settled the whole cowboy clan

started talking about a barbecue down at the river and getting out the guitars, and Faith had to cut them short. She put an arm around Jade and looked up at the cage that hung in the sky and the mountain sitting behind it.

"We have a little more work to do. Let's get these ropes cut."

Chapter 15

Toward Home

They traveled low over the ground, pushing the ivy-covered cage through the air with their minds, until they reached the border between Oregon and Nevada, moving the prison cell just above the tallest structures. The four ropes that had held it in place dangled like boneless legs beneath the box while Clara and Wade complained endlessly. They complained about snakebites, squirrel bites, the speed that jostled them into walls and burned their skin, but mostly they threatened to kill Faith and Dylan when they got out. That was the Quinns: always sure they would come out on top eventually.

At a certain point along the way Faith and Dylan

stopped and tied the jail they'd built between a gathering of tall trees.

"Are you still sure about this?" Dylan asked. "Wouldn't it be safer if we just killed them both?"

It was the second time Dylan had questioned her logic, and this time she offered a deal if he wanted to take it.

"If you really think we should do that, then I'll go along. But I have a condition."

Dylan kicked the ground with the toe of his boot, waited silently until Faith spoke again.

"You have to do it with your bare hands. No hiding behind your pulse. If you're going to kill two people in cold blood, you need to take responsibility for how that's going to feel."

Dylan looked up at the cage thoughtfully, then back at Faith. She secretly hoped he wouldn't take the bait, because she wanted to believe the man she loved couldn't do it, not even to the Quinns.

He surprised her by flying up to the cage and peering inside, and not being able to help herself, she followed. Inside, both Clara and Wade were badly weakened. It would be easy enough to pull them against their will into the ivy and hold them until they stopped breathing.

"I'll open the door for you if this is really what you want," Faith said. "I understand how much they took from you."

For a long moment Dylan stared at the two people who had caused him so much pain. He turned to Faith, put an arm around her, pulled her close.

"Keeping you safe is all I care about. But I can't do it. I won't."

Faith turned into an embrace and they kissed. She touched his battered arms and looked into his eyes, smiling. She didn't have to speak. Dylan knew how she felt. *It makes me happy you couldn't do it.*

"Get a room, losers," Clara said.

Faith and Dylan laughed a little bit at Clara's bitterness and spiraled to the ground, their arms wrapped tightly around each other.

They rested for the night, taking turns watching the cage, and an hour before dawn they moved once more. As the sun came up over the Western State, they found themselves surrounded by an armed air patrol. These soldiers knew by now what they were dealing with in Faith and Dylan—two second pulses, unstoppable— and when they were a mile away from the Western State a negotiation ensued.

"We can't let you any closer than this," a voice said. "Too risky. We don't know what you might do. Our only choice would be to open fire with everything we've got."

The commander was inside the Western State, no doubt sitting next to the president, but he was communicating through a hover drone floating fifty yards away from Faith. A few dozen more armed drones flew like honeybees around the perimeter, along with a whole battalion of Western State troops in jet packs and hovercraft.

Faith observed all the firepower that surrounded her and fairly marveled at the fact that none of it was capable of inflicting so much as a scratch across her skin.

"We don't need to go any closer than this," Faith said. She didn't have to yell over the sound of all the machinery in the air, because it was all whisper-silent tech. "This is far enough."

The commander drone, sheathed in blue with a white star for a nose, proceeded closer.

"You'll need to come inside for processing," the commander said through its crystal-clear audio system. "Will you do that willingly?"

"They do have great technology," Dylan said. "Maybe we could ask for a home theater system and a crate of movies as part of the—"

"Dylan." Faith put up a hand in his face. "I love you, but we've got a few warheads pointing in our direction and some net bombs that could actually complicate this situation. Can we cool it on the jokes for five?"

Dylan wilted comically. "Was I joking?" He'd moved past worrying about ammo pointed in his direction and gone straight to comic relief.

"Just stay here and hold down the fort. Can you do that for me?"

"Get the *Matrix* trilogy and all the *Star Wars* movies in high definition and you got a deal."

Faith rolled her eyes. "It's like working with a nine-year-old."

"And *Star Trek*," Jade added. "The original show, not the movies."

Faith pulled away from Jade and Dylan and hoped the two of them would stay put and keep quiet. When she was close enough to have what could be laughingly called a private conversation, she spoke to the commander of the Western State armed forces.

"I'm Faith Daniels. Behind me are Dylan and Jade Gilmore. We mean you no harm. We've never done anything but try our best to protect you. It's possible that everything we've done will never be known by a single soul in the Western State or any other State system. And we're okay with that. We'd prefer it that way, actually."

The drone stared at Faith, wobbling gently in the sky, like a jagged eye that never blinked. There was no reply.

"We're not like anyone inside. We're different," Faith said, glancing around the space she was floating in. "Obviously you already know that. You're just going to have to trust us when we say we've done some good things for you. We've protected you. And we brought you Prisoner One's two children. Clara and Wade Quinn."

Faith raised her chin to the side, her long blond ponytail jumping softly behind her in the gentle breeze. Clara and Wade hadn't talked for more than an hour, but they talked now.

"She's lying!" Clara screamed, ramming her body into the walls of the ivy cage in abject frustration. It was an act of defiance that must have really hurt given her weakened condition.

"You couldn't hold my father," Wade said defiantly. "You're sure as hell not going to hold us."

The words were hollow, said through the mouth of a boy who had become a very bad man. There was nearly no fight left in the sound of Wade's voice.

Faith looked at the drone as if it really was the commander of the army and she moved close enough to reach out and touch it. "We killed Prisoner One. He's gone. He's not going to cause you any more trouble. And we brought you these two. One of them killed my best friend. The other one killed my parents. They've killed other people we love. And they plotted to kill every living soul in there."

Faith pointed to the Western State and finally a voice emerged from the drone. But it wasn't the commander's this time.

"Ms. Daniels, this is the president of the Western

State. I have before me a report created by a hacker who calls himself Aslan."

"Hawk!" Jade yelled. "He's talking about Hawk!"

Faith turned and put a hand up. *Please, Jade, keep quiet.*

"This report, which appears to be completely valid, contains video and audio files of a kind that we would prefer not to share with the general population of the State system. It traces much of your activity over these many months, including the deaths of your parents, Liz Brinn, Gretchen Quinn, a drifter known only as Clooger, a man named Carl, Meredith Gilmore, and a drifter with a known alias of Glory."

Hearing the names of all the people Faith and Dylan had lost, stacked up neat and tidy like cordwood, took the wind out of Faith. She felt her knees shaking, her mind faltering with the weight of sadness. Dylan came up beside her, then Jade on the other side.

"We've lost a lot of people we love," Dylan said. His voice was strong and firm, the humor gone. "We'd like to get one back, if you don't mind."

"We'll give you the Quinns," Jade said in her defiant way. "We could have just killed them, but we didn't. We could have let them die in the cage. But we don't go around killing people. Even bad people."

Faith got her legs back and started to speak, but the president started in first.

"As I've already said, we are aware of what you've done. And while it flies well outside the bounds of Western State regulations, we're prepared to look the other way. Aslan has agreed to terminate all copies of this report—"

Faith cut him short: "But only if you grant some requests."

There was a lengthy silence on the other end in which Faith could imagine the president of the Western State grinding his teeth and hating the fact that he was being told what to do. When he resumed, he spoke in the same measured tone as before.

"We in turn have agreed to take in these two prisoners and release a recent entry into the State system who goes by the name of Hawk. Finally, we agree to let you leave in peace, to live outside the State system, and to do so without a trace. That is the whole of our arrangement. That is our offer. Do you comply?"

Dylan nudged Faith with his elbow but didn't look at her.

"Seriously?"

She got no answer and felt, in the end, that it couldn't hurt to at least ask.

"There are some movies we'd like to have. And possibly a screen to play them on. And some speakers."

"I've arranged for Hawk to receive a Tablet with every movie and television show on file to date. Commander?"

"Approximately twenty-nine million files, sir."

"I will assume this complies with your viewing pleasure and we are agreed on terms. I must stress, once again: your story can never be told. These records can never be released. And if you should come across this hacker, Aslan, we ask that you allow us the opportunity to speak with him privately."

Did they know Hawk and Aslan were the same person? Somehow Faith thought they probably did. Hawk was undoubtedly smart enough to sever the connection between the two, technically speaking, but the evidence was hard to ignore.

Faith knew, finally, why it was that she could never let herself enter the world of the States. The president hadn't said the words, not exactly. He didn't need to. It was plain as day. *An ignorant society is a safe society. Better they not know they were seconds away from total annihilation.*

"We agree to your terms," Faith said. "We comply."

Faith and Dylan shared what they knew about the care and feeding of two second pulses, including what their weakness was. Four of the larger hovercraft connected to the ropes, holding the ivy cage aloft, taking control of the prison Clay had so expertly created. A hundred flying infantry, with weapons at the ready, surrounded the cage.

"Don't they know all that firepower is useless

against our kind?" Jade asked.

Faith had never heard it said that way—*our kind*—and it made her feel closer to Dylan, Hawk, and Jade than she had before.

"Nope," Dylan said, throwing an arm around Faith as they drifted toward the ground. "They have a lot of faith in conventional weaponry. It's a hard habit to break."

As they landed on the barren, cleared land outside the Western State, the sky began to clear. They watched from a few miles outside the wall as the ivy-covered cage was covered with a camouflage tarp, hiding the strange and dangerous things inside so prying eyes couldn't see it. The glowing wall of the Western State was so big around they couldn't see either end. It vanished on the horizon line, who knew how many miles in either direction.

"God, that thing is getting big," Dylan said. "It'll eat the whole world someday."

"And to think everyone inside could have been killed in an instant. It would have been the biggest graveyard in human history."

"Either that or Zombieland," Jade said in a half whisper.

Dylan and Faith laughed, letting off some of the pressure of the day, and then everything went eerily quiet. The Quinns were gone. The army was gone.

They were alone in what was left of the world outside. Three little souls in the barren world outside the States.

"I've been meaning to ask you," Dylan said, looking down at Jade. "How'd you find your second pulse? Or your first? And why'd you keep the second pulse a secret so long?"

Jade kicked the dirt at her feet and acted as if she didn't know what he was talking about. She'd been holding on to the secret forever and she was still trying to keep it, even after it had escaped into the open. She looked up at him, squinting into the sun, and Faith could see she had found someone she could count on.

"Our mom taught me," Jade said, and Faith was reminded once more: *These two people have the same mom*. "She told me it was a secret, especially the second pulse. She said it was very rare and very powerful." She paused, watching the entry point for the Western State. "She said there would come a day and that I would know. She used to tell me all about it before I fell asleep, when I was little and she came to the lodge more often. She told me I would know it was time to tell for three reasons."

Faith imagined Jade when she was four or five, Meredith telling fairy-tale stories that were all too real.

"The first reason I would know it was time was that you would appear," Jade said. She had shifted her gaze onto Faith. "My mom said you would save the world."

This struck Faith as a strange thing to say, and yet in some ways she did feel like a sacrifice, an open wound the whole world had fallen into.

"What else did she say?" Faith asked, her heart in her throat.

"She said that my brother would be here." Jade looked at Dylan. "She said I could follow him anywhere and he would take care of me. But he wouldn't come for me for a long time."

"You are sort of followable," Faith said, laughing away a tear as she looked at Dylan. "She's right about that. What was the third thing?"

Jade took a deep breath and her brow narrowed, crunching up the soft skin above her eyes.

"She said to keep the secret safe until it could be used on the one man," she said. "He could never know. Not until it was too late."

"Hotspur Chance," Dylan said softly.

Jade's face softened and tears began to pool around her eyes.

"When they took Carl and Clooger, I almost told you both. But I kept hearing my mom's voice. *Not until you can use it on the one man. No matter what.* And before I knew it, it was too late."

"You did a very fine job keeping that secret," Dylan said.

Jade nodded quickly a few times and smiled. "I kept it safe, didn't I?"

Dylan looked at her as big brothers should. "And you saved a hundred and fifty million people. That's what Clooger and Carl worked for all their lives. They didn't die in vain. Not even close."

"We did it together," Jade said.

Faith smiled wistfully, and then she was crying, too. The ache of so much loss, the relief of being finished, these people who were her family—they all mixed together and took her heart to places it had never been, full and broken wide open.

"Sometimes I feel like my heart doesn't fit inside my chest anymore," Faith said.

"Mine, too," Jade agreed.

The entry point for the Western State opened far off in the distance and the HumGee was released into the world. Hawk gunned it, but the HumGee hovered a few inches off the ground, so there was no fishtailing or sliding. His aim was straight and true like an arrow and Jade began walking toward it. She didn't fly or run to Hawk; she just walked.

Faith leaned into Dylan and put her head on his broad shoulder. They watched until the HumGee stopped fifty feet away and Hawk stepped out.

"I guess we're the old couple now," Faith said,

looking contentedly into Dylan's eyes. "Must be nice. I'm worth like a billion dollars."

"Uh-huh."

Hawk and Jade hugged and she planted a serious kiss on his lips that nearly knocked Hawk off his feet. They laughed and smiled and hugged and cried until Faith and Dylan cut the distance between them.

"If you're going to be dating my sister, we're going to need to lay some ground rules," Dylan said.

Hawk came in for a full-on man hug. "Half sister," he corrected.

Faith put an arm around Hawk's shoulder and pulled him in close.

"Aslan? Don't go getting a God complex on me."

Hawk shrugged. "Nah, just needed an alias."

Hawk took Jade gently by the hand and squeezed. She looked at him and wiped her delicate hand under her eyes.

"He likes to hold hands," Jade said.

"Yeah, I know about that." Faith smiled.

Hawk guided Jade to the backseat of the HumGee and glanced at Faith and Dylan. "One of you can drive. I need to spend some time telling Jade about her dad."

Faith wouldn't have thought of it so soon, but Hawk had thought of it. No one knew Clooger better than Hawk. He would tell Jade about how much courage Clooger had, but he would also make him into something more than the military man she knew. It was the most romantic gesture Faith had seen in a long time, and she marveled at Hawk's big heart.

"He's a goof, but he'll put her first," Faith said to Dylan. "She's a lucky girl, your little sister."

"So am I," Dylan said, wrapping his arms around Faith and giving her a long, breathless kiss.

The four of them returned to Timberline Lodge by way of Portland, Oregon. Hawk got his chance to meet some real urban cowboys and listen to Clay tell stories about Carl. They got to have that barbecue by the water, and promised to invite them up to the mountain before the winter set in.

In time Faith Daniels would open each of the locked rooms in her heart, the ones she'd carefully hidden away until a time when she had the strength to open them up and look inside. There was a room for her parents, another for Glory, one for Clooger, one for Liz, one for Dr. Seuss and her lost childhood. So many rooms full of sadness. She would have to open them carefully, slowly, and learn to hold them in a way that wouldn't destroy her. She would need to let the tears come and let the information knock her to her knees and take her breath away.

And hopefully, over time, she would be able to see that the sacrifices made were worth it. She and Dylan and Jade and Hawk would never enter the safety of the States, but they would watch over these things of terrible beauty. They served a purpose she now understood, both symbolic and real. People in the States would hear legend of what they'd done. The story would find its way in; it would live on. It had to, because stories always find the secret way into the hearts and minds of people. And if Wade and Clara ever figured out a way to escape, Faith and Dylan would be waiting; Hawk and Jade, too. They had a place in the broken world they lived in. All that was lost had been worth it.

It had to be.

"If you could go back to the beginning, would you rather I never awakened this thing inside you?" Dylan asked one starry evening.

It was a question not unlike being asked to marry. If she waited too long to answer, the waiting *was* the answer. Dylan was asking Faith many things with that question. Did she trust him? Did she love him? Did she forgive him for changing her into something new without asking her first?

"I would never want to go back," she said, and she meant it. "This is who I am. It's who I always was. I just didn't know it until you showed me."

She felt as she always had for Dylan, but with the darkness that had overshadowed it pushed away on the wind. Dylan threw an arm around her the way he liked

QUAKE ◀ ◀ ◀

to and drew her into a slow walk into the woods.

"Movie night?" he asked. "A little sci-fi action, maybe?"

They'd been back at the lodge for only a few weeks and already Faith had endured a dozen space movies, some of them twice.

"Throw in a romantic comedy and you got a deal," Faith said, looking off into the trees.

Dylan's laugh drifted up into the tree branches overhead.

"Let's get Hawk and Jade in on this, double feature."

It was hard to imagine a time wasn't coming when the Quinns would escape and they'd be drawn back into a conflict they hadn't signed up for. But Faith was finally starting to understand how life worked. You didn't get to choose what the world would require of you. You got to choose only how you responded.

For now, and hopefully for a long time to come, the four of them would make a home at the lodge, way up on the mountain where trouble couldn't find them. Faith and Dylan would explore the woods in the summer, read away the winter with real books from the lodge while the fire roared. They'd watch a lot of old movies and fall asleep in each other's arms.

And that would be more than enough.

273 ◀ ◀ ◀

Acknowledgments

Starting a trilogy is easy, finishing is hard. Many people to thank!

At the top of my list is Katherine Tegen, who deserves many flowers and glasses of champagne for lending her formidable skills to this series. World-class editing, check! Patience, calmness, humor, and grace—check times four! All caps HUG, I can't thank you enough.

For the pro team at HarperCollins. The talent! The passion! The incredible work that puts these books on the map: Lauren Flower, Katie Bignell, Onalee Smith, and Kelsey Horton.

Amy Ryan and Joel Tippie—of all my books these are my favorite covers, and that's saying something.

For Peter Rubie, agent extraordinaire and friend for life. Thank you, buddy.

Lucy Podmore and Rose Brock—Texas is so lucky! Thank you for your incredible encouragement; it means a lot more than you realize.

Squire, Jeremy, and Skip: during the writing of these books we traveled some hard roads together—and hey, we're still kickin'! Thanks, guys.

For Walt, Michael, and Tony. You arrived at a time when I was alone and it made all the difference. GBFL.

And in the end these books are always for Karen, Sierra, and Reece, who make everything possible.